"Qapla'! I am Moklor the Interrogator,"

said the tallest of the Klingons, his very tone an invitation to combat. "What warrior goes there?"

"My name's B'Elanna," she answered.

Moklor's grey eyes narrowed beneath his brow ridge. "Have you come to have your honor challenged?"

She shrugged. "I guess so, yes."

"Are you willing to see the ceremony through to the end?"

"That's the idea, isn't it? What do I do?" B'Elanna asked.

"It will be a lengthy ordeal," the interrogator told her. "First, you must eat from the heart of a sanctified *targ*."

STAR TREK® VOYAGER™

DAY OF HONOR

THE TELEVISION EPISODE

A novel by
Michael Jan Friedman
Based on DAY OF HONOR
Written by Jeri Taylor

POCKET BOOKS
New York   London   Toronto   Sydney   Tokyo   Singapore

This book is a work of fiction. Names, characters, places and incidents are products of the author's imagination or are used fictitiously. Any resemblance to actual events or locales or persons living or dead is entirely coincidental.

An *Original* Publication of POCKET BOOKS

POCKET BOOKS, a division of Simon & Schuster Inc.
1230 Avenue of the Americas, New York, NY 10020

A VIACOM COMPANY

STAR TREK is a Registered Trademark of Paramount Pictures.

This book is published by Pocket Books, a division of Simon & Schuster Inc., under exclusive license from Paramount Pictures.

ISBN: 0-671-01981-3

First Pocket Books printing November 1997

10 9 8 7 6 5 4 3 2 1

POCKET and colophon are registered trademarks of Simon & Schuster Inc.

Printed in the U.S.A.

For Patti,
who had to leave before the second act

DAY OF HONOR

Then: Nineteen Years Ago

CHAPTER
1

FIVE-YEAR-OLD B'ELANNA TORRES SAT IN A CHAIR IN THE center of her parents' great room, a Vulcan puzzle cube in her lap, and tried to make sense of the silence. It wasn't easy.

Her father, a tall, darkly handsome man with friendly brown eyes, was standing by the curved window on one side of the room, staring at something—or at nothing, maybe. B'Elanna couldn't tell.

Her mother, a Klingon with wild red hair and a spirit to match, was sitting at the kitchen table on the other side of the room, picking at a bowl of serpent worms she had prepared moments earlier. She grunted a couple of times, but she didn't seem very hungry.

That was a first. As far back as the girl could remember, her mother had *always* been hungry, even when she was sick with some human disease she didn't have antibodies for.

B'Elanna didn't like the silence, but it was better than the yelling. That had gone on for days, almost every time her parents saw each other. And it had been the worst kind of yelling, a nasty kind that made the girl feel as if she wasn't even there.

After a while, B'Elanna had begun to wonder if she might be the cause of her parents' arguments. She wasn't the ideal child, after all. She had a temper sometimes and she didn't play nicely with the other kids. And though she tried her hardest to make her mother and father proud of her, it didn't always work.

Billy Ballantine, one of the older kids in the colony, had tried to explain it to her. "It's not your fault," he had said. "Your mom's a Klingon. Klingons yell all the time. That's what my dad told me, and he knows just about everything. To a Klingon, he says, yelling is second nature."

B'Elanna was half-Klingon herself, but she hardly knew anything about her mother's people. Her mother seldom spoke of her heritage, and the girl had never met any of her Klingon relatives.

Still, she didn't think Billy Ballantine's father was right. It was only lately that her mother had been yelling. Besides, her mother wasn't the only one raising her voice. B'Elanna's father wasn't Klingon, and he had shouted just as loud as her mother a couple of times.

Anyway, they weren't yelling anymore. B'Elanna wasn't sure, just being a child and all, but she thought that was a good thing. It seemed to her that her parents were calming down, thinking about what they had said and maybe being a little embarassed about it.

Yes. The more she turned that over in her mind, the more it made sense. B'Elanna thought about how things happened sometimes that made her mad, that made her want to yell, and how she needed to be alone for a while afterward to sort it out.

But when a child felt angry about something, she could stomp into her room and close the door. B'Elanna's mother and father shared the same bedroom. It would be silly for one of them to go inside and close the door.

So maybe her parents needed to do other things to be alone. Maybe they needed to hide from each other behind a wall of silence, until they had worked out whatever was bothering them.

And maybe after they were done working things out on their own, maybe they would work things out together—and be happy again. B'Elanna smiled to herself. She would like that. She would like that a lot.

Suddenly, the girl realized she wasn't speeding things up for her parents by sitting there. If she went out and left them alone, they might start talking again a little sooner. Maybe by the time she got back, everything would be normal again, the way it used to be.

Maybe everyone would be happy.

"I'm going out," B'Elanna announced abruptly. She put the puzzle cube away on a wall-shelf meant for such things, and headed for the door.

"Be back before dinner," her mother told her, looking up momentarily from her serpent worms.

"I will," she promised.

"And do not let the Ballantine child fill your head with nonsense," her mother added.

B'Elanna looked at her for a moment. Had her mother heard Billy talking about her—about Klingons? She couldn't tell from the hooded look of her mother's eyes.

"I won't," she replied.

B'Elanna headed for the door, already thinking about what kinds of things she could do outside. But her father's voice stopped her before she could get very far.

"Hey," he said. "I need a hug, Little Bee."

For as long as she could remember, Little Bee had been her father's pet name for her. It made her tingle every time he said it.

"Oh, Daddy," B'Elanna squealed.

She ran to him as fast as she could. At the last possible moment, her father bent down and scooped the girl up in his arms, then hugged her just the way she liked it.

B'Elanna hugged him back, too. She hugged him with all her might, and she was strong for her age. Finally, she let go and he put her down.

The truth was, the girl liked her father a little better than she liked her mother. But of course she wasn't going to tell anyone that. It would only have hurt her mother's feelings.

"See you later," she said—to both of them.

Then she was out the door, running through the glare of the late afternoon sun like a wild animal. For the first time in days, she felt a weight had been lifted off her.

They'll be fine, she told herself. Just wait and see.

B'Elanna's father watched his daughter run out into the bright orange plaza, the sunlight picking highlights out of her soft, brown hair. He found he had a lump in his throat.

Little Bee, he thought sadly.

"You are a coward," his wife spat at him.

He turned to her. Every day, she seemed harder, fiercer, more determined to push him out of her life.

I should have seen it coming a long time ago, he told himself. Hell, I should never have married her in the first place.

"A coward?" he echoed.

He gazed out the window again at his little girl. His Little Bee.

"Yeah," he said. "Maybe I am."

"Hey, B'Elanna!"

The girl turned in the direction of the childish cry and saw Dougie Naismith cutting across the plaza to join her. Dougie was a tall, skinny boy with unruly yellow hair and ears that stuck out from his head.

He was also B'Elanna's best friend.

"What's up?" she asked him.

Dougie pointed to the reddish-orange hills north of the white-domed colony complex. "We found a firechute," he said. "Or really, Erva did. Come on, I'll show you."

B'Elanna looked at him, her pulse pounding all of a sudden. "A firechute? Are you sure?"

The only firechutes she knew were way on the other

side of the world, where the mountains were really big. B'Elanna's father and mother, who worked as geologists for the colony, had shown them to her.

They had taken her into a crack in the earth, a deep, dark one between two towering cliffs. With her hand in her father's and her mother up ahead, lighting the way, the girl had descended along a long, twisting ledge.

At first, she had seen only a ruddy glow that chased the darkness. Then her path came out from behind an outcropping and she got a good look.

B'Elanna remembered the spiraling tongues of ruby-red flame, each as wide around as one of the colony domes and maybe five or six times as high. Of course, that was only the part she could see. According to her father, the fire had traveled a long way before it even entered the crack.

And it wasn't fire, really, though the girl could feel its immense heat on her face, pulling her skin tight across her cheekbones. It was a funny kind of energy that just looked and felt like fire—an energy trapped under the crust of the planet when the world was still forming.

At least, that was the way her father had explained it. All B'Elanna knew was that it was beautiful—so beautiful she couldn't say a word, only stop and gaze in wonder at the spectacle.

So it seemed strange that there could be a firechute in the hills so close to home. No, more than strange. Crazy.

"I'm sure," said Dougie. "Come on, I'll show you."

B'Elanna glanced over her shoulder at her family's house. Her mother hadn't told her her to stick around the colony buildings. She had just said to be back before dinner, and that was at least an hour away.

It occurred to the girl that her parents would be interested in the firechute, too. But if she told them about it, that would distract them from the patching up they needed to do.

Besides, it would be a lot more fun to see the chute for herself, first. She could always show it to her mother and father later.

"All right," she told her friend Dougie. "Let's go."

Together, they set out across the sunbaked flatlands that separated the colony from the hill country. It didn't take long to cross them, either—maybe half an hour at an easy lope. B'Elanna was so excited, she barely felt the afternoon heat.

"I don't get it," she said, as the rust-colored hills loomed in front of them. "Why didn't we ever find anything like this before?"

After all, B'Elanna and her friends had explored the hills many times already. They had found some small caves, but nothing even vaguely resembling a firechute.

"You'll see," was all Dougie would tell her.

It was another couple of minutes before they found Erva Konal. Though she was a year older than Dougie and two years older than B'Elanna, her diminutive size made her look younger than either one of them.

Erva was sitting outside one of the caves they had explored weeks earlier, her thin, delicate features hidden behind patches of sparkling, dark rock dust. Her clothing was covered with the stuff, too.

"It's about time," she said, in her high-pitched

Yrommian voice. "I feel like I've been waiting forever."

"We can't all move as fast as you can," Dougie reminded her.

It was true. Despite their small stature, Yrommians had a funny, ground-eating gait, and Erva was no exception. Try as she might, B'Elanna had never been able to keep up with it.

"So where's the firechute?" B'Elanna asked.

Erva jerked her head in the direction of the cave. "In here," she said. Then she got up and went inside.

B'Elanna shook her head as she followed the Yrommian into darkness. "This isn't a joke, is it?"

"No joke," Dougie confirmed. He was right behind B'Elanna as they headed for the depths of the cavern. "I know we were in this cave before and everything, but this time we saw something in the back of it."

"Like a flash of light," Erva explained.

"We found an opening in the rock," the boy added. "It was too narrow for me to get through, but not too narrow for Erva."

"Come on," said the Yrommian. "I'll show you. Just watch your head. The ceiling gets pretty low here."

B'Elanna couldn't see well in the darkness, but she managed to keep track of Erva. Her friend got down on her hands and knees, then gestured for B'Elanna to do the same.

"I wish I could go with you," Dougie sighed.

"Maybe we'll find another chute," the Yrommian suggested. "One a little easier to get to."

"Yeah," said the boy. "Right."

B'Elanna felt Erva's hand on her arm. The Yrommian's fingers were cold, but that was normal for her people.

"It's this way," she said—and slipped forward into the darkness.

Suddenly, B'Elanna couldn't feel her friend's hand anymore. It was gone. "Erva?" she said.

She moved forward herself and extended her hand. It brushed against a rough, hard wall of stone. She moved it to the right—more stone. Then she moved it to the left.

And found an opening. The one that Erva must have gone through.

"Let's go, already," said a high-pitched voice.

With a little care, B'Elanna figured out the dimensions of the opening. It was about three feet high, but very narrow. So narrow, in fact, that she was sure she wouldn't fit through.

"What are you waiting for?" asked her friend.

"I think I may be too big," B'Elanna told her.

"Nonsense. Give it a try."

B'Elanna did as Erva told her. It was a tight fit, all right—but in the end, she *did* fit through. As she dragged her legs out of the hole, she could see the opening outlined in the faint, gray light from the cave mouth.

"You made it!" Erva cheered.

B'Elanna looked around. She couldn't see anything in the darkness ahead of her, not even the Yrommian. "Now what?" she asked.

"Now we wait," her friend told her.

But they didn't have to wait for long. The words were barely out of Erva's mouth when the place lit up with a blood-red light. And in that sudden flood of illumination, B'Elanna saw a thin lash of ruby flame emerge from a hole in the cavern floor.

It wasn't a small hole, either. It was half the size of the cavern itself, and this cavern was even bigger than the one outside.

The lash of flame died down, but not the blood-red glow. That lingered, meaning the fire hadn't subsided completely. It just wasn't visible from where they sat.

B'Elanna looked at her friend. "You weren't kidding," she said.

"Of course not," Erva told her.

Then she started to move, her shadow looming large and dancing wildly on the cavern wall behind her. It seemed to B'Elanna that her friend was inching forward, trying to get a better view of the chute.

But after a moment, she realized Erva was doing more than that. She was moving to the side as well, where a narrow ledge circumvented the pit and connected with the cavern floor on the other side.

"What are you doing?" B'Elanna asked her.

"I'm going to the other side," the Yrommian explained. "It's lower there, and there's less of a lip. I'll get a better view."

"But it's dangerous," B'Elanna protested.

"Only if the flame dies down before I get there and it becomes dark." Her friend winked at her. "And if I hurry, that won't happen."

Before B'Elanna could stop her, Erva had gotten to her feet and sidled out onto the ledge. Pressing her back into the cavern wall, the Yrommian made her way along the side of the chute.

B'Elanna watched, spellbound. The ruddy light coming up from the hole in the earth made Erva seem ruddy as well. Her hair gleamed like Klingon blood-wine, her eyes like dying suns.

"What's going on in there?" Dougie called from the next cavern. His voice echoed from one wall of the chute to the other. "I *hate* not being able to get in to see!"

You might not want to see *this,* B'Elanna thought. If Erva fell off the ledge, she would die. There was no question about it.

But the Yrommian didn't seem the least bit afraid. If anything, she seemed giddy with her nearness to the fire, all possibility of fear swept away in a tide of delight.

"Come on," said Dougie. "Somebody *talk* to me."

"Erva's going over to the other side," B'Elanna answered.

"The other side?"

"Of the chute," she added.

Dougie didn't say anything for a moment. "How?" he asked finally.

B'Elanna frowned. "She's walking."

"She can do that?"

"I guess," the girl said, trying to keep the doubt out of her voice.

Erva took a step, then slid. Another step, and slid some more. Little by little, she approached the far side of the cavern. Finally, to B'Elanna's surprise and elation, her friend came within a step or two of her goal.

Suddenly, without warning, the firechute filled with a rush of energy. The flame bounded off the ceiling and folded back on itself like a great and terrible blossom, turning the cavern a hideous red with its fury. B'Elanna closed her eyes and pressed herself as far back into the stone as she could go.

But the fire found her.

She felt its searing energy on her face, scorching her skin and superheating the air she drew into her throat, making her cry out with the pain. For a moment, she thought she had been burned beyond recognition, both inside and out.

Then the heat and the light diminished, and B'Elanna opened her eyes and felt her face with a terrible urgency. But to her surprise, her skin was still smooth, still in one piece. The burn she had sustained was no worse than the ones she got from being in the sun too long.

Swallowing, B'Elanna saw that her throat was okay too. Gathering her courage, she gazed across the chute.

She was prepared for the worst—prepared to find that Erva had fallen into the hole, or been burned to ashes by her nearness to the fire. But neither of those things had happened.

The Yrommian was on the other side of the chute, huddled against the cavern wall. She had wrapped her arms about herself and was trembling like a *naiga* spore in a strong wind, moaning in a kind of singsong rhythm.

But as far as B'Elanna could tell, her friend was all right. She hadn't been burned any worse than B'Elanna herself.

She licked her lips. "Erva?"

B'Elanna's voice echoed a bit. But it was still intelligible when it reached the Yrommian.

Erva turned away from the cavern wall and peered at B'Elanna with eyes red from crying. "I'm still here," she said with some surprise.

"For now," B'Elanna told her. "But you've got to get out of there. The next time, the fire might be worse."

It was true. Her parents had said that about fire-chutes. Just when you thought you had seen one at its worst, it got even fiercer.

Her friend shook her head, squeezing out tears between swollen eyelids. "I can't," she whimpered.

"You've *got* to," B'Elanna insisted.

But it was no use.

CHAPTER
2

B'ELANNA SHOOK HER HEAD. THE YROMMIAN WASN'T making a move to help herself—even if it meant her death. She was just too frightened.

There was only one other possibility, the half-Klingon girl told herself. Only one other way to get her friend Erva out of her predicament—and that was to go all the way over and get her.

She took a look into the chute, where flame after twisting flame was emerging from its depths. There was no time to lose. The longer B'Elanna waited, the better the chance that the flames would shoot up again, turning both her and her friend into ashes.

Taking a ragged breath, she ventured out onto the narrow precipice. She took a sideways step. Then another. And another.

With each one, she got a little closer to Erva. She focused on that, forgetting about everything else. All she had to do was get one step closer each time and she would be all right.

"I'm coming," she said, to steady her own nerves as much as her friend's. "I'll be there before you know it."

As if in response, a tongue of flame rose high enough to lick at B'Elanna's feet. Clenching her jaw shut, she waited until it subsided, then continued along the ledge.

She had come halfway, she estimated. It was a milestone, something she could build a hope on. If she could come halfway, she could make it all the way across.

And if she could make it across one way, she could get back.

It sounded good, B'Elanna told herself. But even as she thought it, she knew there were no guarantees. This time, there weren't any adults around to help her out. If everything came out all right, it would be because of her and no one else.

She smiled at the idea. Her parents would be proud of her then. They couldn't be anything else. And they would love her so much, they would forget about their quarreling.

B'Elanna slid her right foot sideways, then followed with the left. Right, then left. Right, left . . . always certain to test her footing before she put any weight down.

Things would be good again, she told herself. She pictured herself as a baby in her parents' embrace, just the way she had seen it in the family holos. As she brought her right foot forward, she imagined the feel of her parents' arms around her, firm and reassuring.

Left foot now, B'Elanna thought. But as she moved it, she could feel it slip off what she had believed was solid rock.

And keep going.

For a long, terrible second, she thought she felt herself falling, dropping dizzily into the searing embrace of the flames. Then she threw herself back into the cavern wall as hard as she could.

The impact jarred B'Elanna to the roots of her teeth, but it kept her from going over. And before she could topple again, she found purchase with her left foot and lifted herself up.

Her heart was pounding so hard it was difficult to breathe, much less to continue along the ledge. So she waited a moment, taking long, deep breaths, until she was calm enough to go on.

Strangely enough, the going was much easier after that. It was as if B'Elanna had confronted the worst that could happen, and after that nothing seemed quite so scary anymore.

Finally, she reached the other side of the cavern floor, where her friend Erva was staring at her wide-eyed. It wasn't as if she wasn't glad to see B'Elanna. In fact, she was very glad.

But she knew that, having reached her, B'Elanna would want to take her back. And Erva was still about as afraid of that as she could be.

"It's all right," B'Elanna told her friend. She knelt beside Erva and put her hand on the Yrommian's shoulder. "You got here, right? That means you can get back."

Erva shook her head. "No, it doesn't. I'm too scared, B'Elanna, too scared even to *move.*"

B'Elanna glanced into the pit, where the tongues of crimson flame seemed to be lengthening each time they shot up. "If you don't move," she explained, "you'll die here, Erva."

"Then I'll die!" the Yrommian screamed.

"And I'll die *with* you!" B'Elanna shouted back. "Because I'm not leaving you here. Either we both go back or neither of us does."

She didn't know what made her say that. She sure hadn't had that in mind when she set out to rescue Erva. But as soon as the words came out, she was glad they had—because they made a change in her friend.

It was one thing for Erva to sacrifice her own life because she was afraid. But to sacrifice B'Elanna's life as well—that was something else again.

The muscles worked in the Yrommian's little jaw. A light showed in her eyes. "All right," she said. "We'll do it."

B'Elanna nodded. "Together."

And they did.

They made their way back along the entire ledge, Erva's hand clasping B'Elanna's in a white-knuckled grip. They didn't slip, either. They didn't even come close to slipping. The two of them just took their time and managed to ignore the fire raging in the pit in front of them.

When they reached the other side, they fell to their knees, thankful and relieved that they had made it. As they pulled themselves up again to make their way out of the cavern, B'Elanna took a last look back. Then Erva slipped through the crack in the wall and her friend wriggled after her.

It was just in time, too. Because a moment later, the

crimson geyser of energy erupted again—this time, with an intensity B'Elanna hadn't imagined possible. Even from the next cavern, she could see its brilliance and feel the heat of it blistering her skin.

If she and Erva had remained in the chute-cavern any longer, they would have been burned to cinders. But they had escaped.

"Wow!" said Dougie. "That was something!"

Erva nodded. "Something," she echoed.

B'Elanna smiled wearily. Her friend was safe and sound, and so was she. No one had gotten hurt.

And as a bonus, she had a tale of bravery to tell her parents.

B'Elanna's mother stood beside her bed, in the bedroom she and her husband shared, and considered the jewel-encrusted object in her hand. It was a *jinaq* amulet, worn by Klingon maidens from the day they came of age—a signal that they were ripe for conquest.

She hadn't worn it since her wedding day, when she had vowed to honor and cherish her human husband. Those vows seemed hollow now, the words of a fool. But no matter what happened, she wouldn't wear the amulet again.

She was no maiden, after all. And she never intended to leave herself open again for conquest.

Suddenly, she heard the front door swing open. Her first thought was that her husband had come back. Then she realized it was her daughter, and she steeled herself for what was ahead.

B'Elanna's voice was shrill with enthusiasm as she

called from the next room. "Mama? Daddy? You'll never guess what happened!"

"In here," said her mother, her throat as dry as the ground outside the colony buildings.

A moment later, the girl burst into the room, her face flushed beneath a layer of rock dust. "Mama," B'Elanna cried, "you're not going to believe it! I saved Erva's life! She and Dougie were exploring the caverns out north by the mines and they found a firechute! Then Erva got stuck in the cavern with the chute and—"

It was then that her daughter seemed to realize something was wrong. B'Elanna met her mother's gaze and seemed to see the anger that the woman held clenched within her. The anger—and the shame.

"Mama?" she said tentatively. "Is something wrong?"

Her mother didn't answer. She had called her husband a coward not so long ago, but now she discovered the same cowardice in herself.

B'Elanna came over and embraced her. "There *is* something the matter, isn't there? Tell me, Mama. What is it?"

Her mother looked past her, nostrils flaring. She was a Klingon. It was her duty to say what there was to say, good or bad. Still, she found it difficult to speak, and it irked her that it should be so.

You've been living among humans too long, she thought bitterly. They've made you weak and sentimental.

Suddenly, B'Elanna knew without being told. Her mother could see it in her eyes. "It's Daddy," the girl whispered.

There, her mother thought. Your duty has been done for you, *p'tahk*. "Your father is leaving us," she said. "In some ways, he is already gone."

B'Elanna didn't understand. "Where is he, Mama?" Her little girl's voice was little more than a whimper.

Her mother jerked her head in the direction of the front door. "Making arrangements at the administration office. There is a ship coming by in a few days. He will be on it when it departs."

"But why?" asked B'Elanna, still numb, still disbelieving. "Why would Daddy want to go somewhere else?"

Her mother shook her head, her long red tresses sweeping her shoulders. When she spoke, her words were like knives, cutting them both.

"You will have to ask him that yourself, child."

It can't be, B'Elanna thought.

She ran across the plaza in the direction of the administration building, her breath rasping in her throat, her heart pounding from more than her exertion.

It can't be, the girl repeated. It's not fair.

She had thought she was going to make her father proud of her. She had imagined he would listen to her story and tell her how brave she was, and want to stay with her forever and ever. But now her father was going to leave anyway, no matter *how* brave she had been.

It hurt to think that. It hurt worse than the energy in the chute. B'Elanna wanted to cry, but she couldn't. Other people cried, but not Klingons or even half-Klingons. She had learned that early on.

Suddenly, she caught sight of him. Her father was coming out of the administration dome, his eyes downcast. Then some sixth sense told him to look up and he saw her.

He tried to smile, but he didn't get very far. His eyes stayed sad, no matter what the rest of his face did.

"Oh, Daddy," B'Elanna said, and leaped into his arms.

"Little Bee," he whispered in her ear, clasping her to him. "How did you get so dirty?"

"You can't leave," she told him. "You can't. Not after I was so brave. Not after I saved Erva in the cavern."

He held her away from him. "What?"

B'Elanna told him all about it, barely taking a breath. The whole story spilled out in a matter of moments.

"So you *can't* leave," she insisted. "Not after I've been so good. And I can be good like that *all* the time."

Her father shook his head, tears welling in his eyes. "I wish it was that simple," he said. "I really do."

"But it *can* be that simple," B'Elanna argued. "All you have to do is tell the administrator you've changed your mind—or made a mistake or something. You want to stay home with me and Mama."

Her father swallowed. She could see his Adam's apple move up and down in his throat. "Come on," he said softly. "We can go home for now, at least, Little Bee."

B'Elanna looked into his eyes. They were still sad,

still wet with human tears. "But not for good," she said. "Right?"

He didn't answer for a moment. It seemed to her it hurt him too much to answer. But eventually, he found the words.

"Not for good," he sighed at last.

For a moment, the girl got angry. She didn't want her father to go away—and she was his daughter, wasn't she? Why couldn't he just stay and do what made her happy?

As if he had read her mind, he said, "You'll get over it, Little Bee. You'll be happy again. And so will your mother. Just remember that and it'll happen before you know it."

"But how can I be happy," she asked, "without you?"

Even before she could get all the words out, she was overcome by the need to hug him again. She hugged her Daddy long and hard, harder than she had ever hugged him before. And when she was done, he took her hand and they walked back to their dome.

A couple of days later, he was gone, just the way her mother said he would be. And B'Elanna and her mother were all alone.

Then: One Year Ago

Agron Lumas walked out onto his balcony and surveyed the tawny hills of the Konoshin river valley. The rays of the late afternoon sun slanted across the tableau, making white-hot points of the pollen clusters rising from the *treybaga* trees lining each slope.

It was a sight few on his world could afford. But then, Lumas was successful at his profession. He had earned his perquisites in life.

Smiling at the notion, he breathed in and then out. It was the growing season. The air was sweet. And for the first time in what seemed like a long time, he had a few minutes all to himself.

After all, Lumas's workday was over, and the stringed-instrument concert up the mountain wasn't slated to begin for half a decacycle. His wife and two daughters, who would normally have been buzzing about the great room like insects, were still downstairs selecting clothes for the occasion.

Lumas chuckled to himself. His elder daughter, Finaea, meant to impress a young man who would be playing the chinharp. He knew this because she had told him so. Hence, the fuss over which outfit to wear.

Of course, Lumas's wife outwardly disapproved of Finaea's obsession with the lad. That was only proper. But it didn't stop her from reveling in the opportunity to dress her daughter up.

Suddenly, something occurred to Lumas. He could stand on his balcony any time he wished. But with the great room empty, he had a rare chance to try out the new realizor his wife had purchased.

Yes, he thought. This is the perfect time to try it out.

Re-entering the great room, with its strategically positioned works of two-dimensional art, Lumas brushed his fingers against the sensor on his western wall. Instantly, the portals in the room irised down to nothing. A brush of an adjacent sensor and the overhead lights dimmed, leaving the vast chamber dark and deliciously expectant.

Next, Lumas approached the stand in the corner of the room, where the realizor band sat in its simple metal cradle. Picking up the device, he admired its sleek, black lines. Then he placed it over his head.

The realizor was so light, he barely knew it was there. But then, this was a state-of-the-art unit, and its physical attributes were only the smallest part of the advantages it offered.

Lumas touched his finger to one of the studs on the side of the band, activating its creator function. A tap on a second stud notified the mechanism that he wasn't seeking anything permanent.

Only a moment's diversion—it was all Lumas had time for. But even that might turn out to be immensely satisfying, if all he had heard about this realizor was true.

Closing his eyes, he pictured a sculpture garden he had visited in Changor Province a year or so before. He recalled the way the willowy pieces of molded metal had glinted in the light of the twin moons, swaying and turning under the influence of an insistent sea breeze.

Beautiful, he thought. Unutterably beautiful.

Then Lumas opened his eyes and saw that the sculptures had invaded his great room. The place was filled with them. And though there were neither moons nor sea breezes present, the sculptures rolled and undulated just as they had that evening in Changor.

Lumas heard a sound: laughter, he thought, childlike and uninhibited. Then, with a thrill of surprise, he realized it was coming from his own throat—and laughed some more.

But then, who wouldn't have laughed? Who wouldn't have been delighted by such an experience? Lumas had recreated the sculpture garden with impeccable verisimilitude and vivid detail. It was even more than he had hoped for.

He reminded himself to congratulate his wife on her purchase. This was worth every gem note she had paid for it.

"Father?" said a voice, high and thin.

"Agron?" said another—that of an adult.

Lumas turned and saw that his family had entered the great room. They were standing at the other end of the chamber, their eyes wide with wonder at what he had made.

"Why," said Finaea, "it's wonderful." She turned to Lumas. "Did you make this yourself, Father?"

He nodded, pleased that his daughter should approve. It had been a long time since any of his works had made her smile. But then, that was only normal when it came to budding adults.

Lumas's wife ran her fingers along a delicate limb of one of the sculptures. She smiled. "I didn't know this place had had such a profound effect on you. But I see now how beautiful it must have seemed."

More so to him than to her, he realized now. Strange that that should be so, after they had been mates for so long. Yet there it was.

"Can I add something?" asked Lumas's younger daughter, Anyelot. "A stream, maybe? Or a walkway?"

He grinned. Anyelot would be an architect some day. There was no doubt of that. He reached out to touch her brow with his fingertips.

Then something happened—something he found alarming. Suddenly, Lumas and his loved ones weren't alone in the swaying sculpture garden.

Suddenly, there were three other figures.

Their skin was pasty-pale, their bodies encased in hard black harnesses. Instead of hands, they displayed mechanical appendages. Tubes sprouting from their chests ended in connections to their hairless skulls.

The strangers' faces were even more disturbing— that is, the part that could be seen. Half of each visage was concealed behind a mysterious black prosthetic. The other half was cold, expressionless, yet for all that driven by some arcane purpose.

Lumas didn't understand. He hadn't asked the realizor to create these beings. To his knowledge, he had never even seen anything like them.

Yet there they were. And if they were chilling to him, he could only imagine what his wife and daughters were feeling.

"Father . . . ?" Anyelot whimpered, her voice climbing in pitch. "What *are* these things? Make them go away!"

"Don't worry," Lumas told her, his voice sounding strange to him with the band on his head. "They'll be gone in a moment, little one."

All it would take was an effort of will. Lumas stared at the strangers and wished them into oblivion.

But nothing happened. The creatures remained. One of them even went so far as to grab his wife's wrist—and since the realizor's creations had substance, she couldn't pull it back again.

"Help me!" she cried, with genuine panic in her voice.

Lumas didn't know what to do. He had never heard of anything like this happening before. A realizor was supposed to be attuned to its wearer's whims, completely and utterly. It wasn't supposed to *defy* him.

Chilled to his core, Lumas reached up and tore the band off his head. As he threw it to the floor, the sculpture garden wavered and vanished. But the nightmare beings remained.

Only then did Lumas get a glimpse of the truth. The invaders had nothing to do with the realizor. They weren't products of his imagination. They existed on their own, just like him and his wife and his daughters.

In short, they were *real*.

As Lumas watched, one of them pulled Finaea to him and embraced her—but not as the youth who played the chinharp would have embraced her. The invader's grip was powerful, stifling—unyielding.

"No!" Lumas shouted.

But it didn't come out as the bellow of rage he had intended. It emerged as little more than a murmur, a sigh.

Lumas lunged at the invader, intending to rip his arm off if need be—anything to free his baby, his treasure. But he barely shuffled forward. His legs felt leaden, useless, his hands little more than lumps of flesh at the ends of his arms.

Of course, Lumas thought, in a still-rational part of his mind. It was an aftereffect of the realizor. It always took several seconds for the wearer to regain full use of his faculties.

"Agron!" his wife cried. "Please, it's hurting me!"

He tried to move again, but he was still too weighted down. As he looked on, horrified beyond measure, Anyelot flung herself at the intruder who had grabbed her mother—but she couldn't pry open that viselike grip.

Then Anyelot, too, was seized—in her case, by the back of the neck. The deathly pale stranger raised her off her feet, choking her, seemingly oblivious to the croaking sounds coming from her throat or the frantic kicking of her legs.

"Leave me alone!" Anyelot bawled. "Leave me alone!"

It didn't help. It was as if her tormentor hadn't even heard her.

Lumas felt hot tears streaming down his face. A second time, he attempted to push himself forward, but couldn't move his feet quickly enough. So instead of lunging, he simply fell.

He lay there on the floor as his wife screamed for him. As Finaea screamed for him. As little Anyelot screamed for him, twisting desperately in the grasp of her silent captor.

How could this be? Lumas asked himself. How? Was it his fault? Had he somehow *inflicted* this fate on them?

"Agron!" his wife shrieked—and reached out for him.

Lumas had accomplished one thing with his fall—he was closer to her now. Close enough, perhaps, to grasp her hand. Lifting his own, he fought his paralysis and stretched it to within inches of her fingers.

Their eyes met. Lumas saw something dark and hideous in hers, something more than terror and loathing. It was as if the intruder had somehow begun to infect her with his darkness.

Feeling control flooding back into his limbs, he reached still further—and grasped his wife's hand. But as he did this, her fingers went limp, and the light left her eyes altogether.

Still he held on, unwilling to give her up, unwilling to surrender. That was when her captor pulled her away from him and raised a mechanical appendage. Lumas tried to roll out of the way, but it was too late.

The appendage came down across his head with a force he couldn't have imagined. He felt himself falling into a deep, dark emptiness—though it wasn't nearly as great as the emptiness of loss inside him.

When he woke, some time later, his world was in flames.

Now

CHAPTER

1

B'ELANNA TORRES, CHIEF ENGINEER OF THE *STARSHIP Voyager*, found herself standing in the center of a large, redstone plaza, the sky above her dark and dusky and vibrating with desert heat.

A hot, gritty wind caressed her face as she looked around. The circle of arches surrounding the plaza looked as if they had been carved from solid rock. But for all their majesty, they were no more impressive than the tall, rough-hewn structure that rose beside her, a flat, metal gong in the shape of a hexagon hanging from its only protrusion.

As B'Elanna watched, a tongue of pale flame leaped from the structure's goblet-shaped top. Turning to smoke, it twisted on the wind and vanished.

Suddenly, she saw movement. A powerful, bare-chested figure appeared on either side of the plaza.

Each one was armed with a *lirpa*—an ancient weapon with a curved blade on one end and a heavy bludgeon on the other.

The wind blew again, leaching moisture from B'Elanna's every pore. She had only been here a few seconds and she was already beginning to sweat.

She knew this place—or rather, not the place itself, but its type. It was the sort of age-old temple one might find on Vulcan, where the indigenous race's once-tumultuous nature had been tamped down under centuries of severe mental discipline.

But here, in this primitive place of worship, surrounded by ocher-colored wastes and the vague black shapes of far-off mountains, the prospect of violence was still very much alive. B'Elanna glanced again at the figures holding the *lirpas*. A half-Klingon by birth, she had never before appreciated how much Vulcans and her mother's people had in common.

Still, she hadn't come to this setting of her own free will. When B'Elanna arrived at the holodeck a couple of minutes earlier, she had called up a new program she had been building from the inside out. Or anyway, she *thought* she had called it up.

But her new program involved cool, dank caves and chill mists—not a hot, arid desert that looked for all the world like an open wound. And it certainly didn't contain Vulcans.

No matter, she told herself. Anybody can make a mistake. She simply called for the half-finished cave program again. Then she closed her eyes and inhaled, anticipating a breath of subterranean cold.

What she got was another torrid wind playing over her face, with a familiarity she was beginning not to like. B'Elanna opened her eyes and saw that nothing had changed. She was still standing in the middle of the Vulcan temple, heat waves rising off the stone all around her.

There was only one explanation. The holodeck was malfunctioning. This wasn't good news, considering how much *Voyager*'s crew depended on the ship's holodecks.

Sighing, she said, "Computer, terminate program."

Abruptly, the temple and the Vulcan desert around it vanished. They were replaced by an intricate network of electromagnetic field emitters and omnidirectional holodiodes—the devices that enabled the holodeck to create and sustain its illusions.

"Well," B'Elanna breathed, "at least *that* command still works."

As she walked toward the exit, a pair of interlocking doors automatically slid away from each other. The engineer could see the corridor beyond them, where the holodeck controls lurked beyond the bulkhead.

B'Elanna knew she didn't have the time to do a thorough repair job. Eventually, she would have to turn it over to someone else. Nonetheless, she pulled away the appropriate bulkhead panel and started diagnosing the problem.

After all, on a ship like *Voyager,* there was always too much to do and not enough time in which to do it. If she didn't tackle each difficulty as it came up, she would soon be deluged.

Worse, B'Elanna would have to explain that deluge to the captain—and that was *not* her idea of a good time.

* * *

Tom Paris found the object of his search in the corridor outside the ship's holodeck: she had taken a bulkhead plate off and was tinkering with the controls located behind it.

"Morning," he said.

Paris had learned not to approach B'Elanna without giving her sufficient warning. The one time he had done that, he had gotten a couple of bruised ribs for his trouble.

The engineer glanced at him. "Morning," she replied. Then she went back to her work.

Stopping alongside her, he propped his hand against the bulkhead. Then he peered over her shoulder at the holodeck's control mechanisms.

"Mm," Paris said judiciously. "That doesn't look good."

"It's *not* good," B'Elanna agreed, without sparing him another glance. Suddenly, she straightened, causing him to straighten, too. "Unfortunately, I don't have the time to devote to it right now."

"Oh?" said Paris.

"I've got an emergency shutdown drill in engineering a few minutes from now." Picking up the bulkhead plate, she put it back in its place. "So someone else will have to fix this—when they can find the time."

"Too bad," he commented. "I was hoping to use the holodeck this evening."

"For what?" B'Elanna asked.

"Dinner," said Paris. "For two."

She gave him her trademark look—a half-scowl, half-smile that never failed to fascinate the hell out of him. "Dinner," she echoed.

He nodded. "With you."

The engineer rolled her eyes. "I'm too busy, Tom." She started down the corridor, all business.

He caught up to her, then created an imaginary vista with a sweep of his hand. "Picture it, B'Elanna. A table for two, on a plateau high above the Yrommian rain forest. The setting sun dissolving in a rising sea of mists. A cool breeze caressing your bare shoulders . . ."

She waved away the suggestion. "One doesn't bare one's shoulders near an Yrommian rain forest, Tom. Not unless one wants to be a meal for a horde of *gorada* flies."

He shrugged. "I've never had any problems with them."

"You're not half-Klingon," B'Elanna reminded him. "Those gorada flies like *hot*-blooded species."

"And you think your blood's hotter than mine?" Paris asked frankly.

She met his gaze. "I'd say that's a conversation for another time, wouldn't you?" Coming to a turbolift, she stepped inside.

He followed her. "Okay. Forget about our blood temperatures. Let's go back to the dinner discussion."

"That was a discussion?" B'Elanna asked, as the lift doors closed behind them. "Don't you think that's a bit of an exaggeration?"

"There you go again," Paris told her.

The engineer's eyes narrowed. "There I go what?"

"There you go folding your arms," he said. "That's body language for 'I'm scared stiff of you.'"

B'Elanna looked down and saw her arms woven tightly across her chest. She unwove them immediately. Then she made a point of staring into Paris's eyes almost belligerently.

"You're out of your mind," she told him. "I'm not frightened of you or anyone else." She rubbed her arm with one of her hands. "For your information, I'm a little chilly, that's all."

He grinned at her. "A nice warm mudbath could take care of that. When the holodeck is fixed, of course."

"And I suppose you'd be willing to share it with me," B'Elanna surmised.

"Well," said Paris, "I could be persuaded."

"You never give up, do you?"

"Never," he confirmed.

She sighed. "Look, tonight's not a possibility. But how about tomorrow night? That is, if nothing ridiculous comes up."

Paris spread his hands expansively. "Tomorrow it is." Suddenly, he remembered. "Hey, isn't tomorrow the Day—"

"—of Honor. Yes, it is." B'Elanna glanced at him. "In fact, I've been working on a holodeck program to celebrate it."

"My," he said, "we *have* come a long way. Last year, you wanted to run and hide on the Day of Honor."

"Well," she replied, "last year's Day of Honor was a little better than all the others. Hence, the program. Actually, I was going to shape it up a little, but then I discovered the holodeck was on the blink."

That gave Paris an idea. "Listen, you're so busy and all—why don't I shape up the program for you? That is, when the holodeck's fixed."

B'Elanna looked skeptical. "You?"

"Why not? I probably know as much about Klingons as you do. And what I don't know, I could look up."

"I don't know," she said.

"Hey," Paris declared, "what have you got to lose?"

Just then, the doors opened. As B'Elanna exited the lift, he accompanied her. After all, he wasn't due on the bridge for another couple of hours.

"So what do you say?" Paris asked. "It'll give us a chance to do something creative together. And you'll enjoy the program more if there's an element of surprise . . . right?"

She stopped in the middle of the corridor, exasperated. "Fine, Tom. Complete the program." As she looked at him, her gaze softened. "I mean, I appreciate the sentiment and everything. Just don't do anything I wouldn't do, all right?"

"No problem," he assured her.

Then Paris watched her walk the rest of the way to engineering. The doors slid open as B'Elanna approached, and then closed behind her, depriving him of her company.

The flight controller sighed. He'd had trouble with a lot of things in life, but the opposite sex wasn't one of them. He had always had a knack for attracting women and keeping them attracted.

What's more, he wasn't sure B'Elanna was any exception. But if she *was* attracted to him, she sure had a funny way of showing it. Even arranging a dinner date was like pulling teeth.

Of course, he mused, that only made her more desirable to him.

Ensign Harry Kim stopped in front of his friend's quarters and waited for the door sensors to register his presence. A moment later, he heard Paris's voice: "Come on in."

As the door slid aside, Kim entered. He found the flight controller sitting at the computer terminal in his living room, staring at the monitor.

"What's so interesting?" Kim asked.

He peered over Paris's shoulder to get a look at the screen. It displayed a line drawing of a monstrous being with Klingon features.

"Fek'lhr?" he said, reading the name underneath the illustration.

His friend frowned. "A mythical beast, the guardian of *Gre'thor*—which is about as close as Klingons get to hell and the devil."

Kim nodded. "Interesting." But, now that he thought about it, not really Paris's cup of tea. He said so.

"True," said Paris, leaning back in his chair. "That is, until today. Suddenly, I have a burning desire to know more about Klingon culture."

Kim smiled. "And why is that?"

Paris looked at him apologetically. "It's kind of confidential. At least, I think it is."

"But it has something to do with B'Elanna," Kim guessed.

"What makes you say that?"

"Oh, I don't know," Kim said. "Maybe the fact that she's the only one in the entire quadrant with a

Klingon heritage. Or the fact that you have a poorly disguised interest in her. Or the fact that, as I recall, tomorrow is that holiday she used to hate."

Paris grunted. "The Day of Honor."

"Yeah, that one."

The flight controller regarded him. "Harry, my man, you've become quite the detective. You know that?"

"So that *is* what this is about," Kim deduced.

Paris held his ground. "Can't say. It's confidential. And besides, B'Elanna would kill me if she knew I'd told anyone about this."

Swiveling his monitor around, he tapped out a new command on his keyboard. The image on the screen changed. Now *Fek'lhr* was a fully fleshed-out figure placed in a cavern setting.

"Very nice," Kim said. "What is it?"

"You're the detective," his friend answered. "You tell me."

The ensign shrugged. "The basis of a holodeck program?"

Paris's eyes widened. "You're better than I thought."

Kim stroked his chin. "A holodeck program . . . to commemorate the Day of Honor. That's it, right?"

The flight controller put his arm behind him and pretended someone was twisting it. "You forced it out of me," he rasped.

The ensign nodded. "And it's a surprise?"

"Not really. B'Elanna started it. I'm just adding some finishing touches for her. You think she'll like *Fek'lhr?*"

Kim winced. "You might want to tone him down a little."

Paris swiveled the monitor back and took another look. "I think you may be onto something." He tapped out another command on the keyboard. "There we go. A little less *Fek'lhr*ish."

"Anyway," said Kim, "I came here to ask you something."

His friend was squinting as he considered his creation. "Fire away, Harry. What's on your mind?"

The ensign told him. "Actually," he explained, "it was Bandiero's idea. But it sounds like fun."

"That it does," Paris agreed. "Count me in. Just let me know when."

"Will do," said Kim, his mission accomplished. He patted the flight controller on the shoulder. "Good luck with *Fek'lsh.*"

"Fek'lhr," Paris said, correcting him.

The ensign chuckled. "Whatever."

Then, leaving his friend to his Klingon enterprise, Kim turned down the corridor and headed for Neelix's quarters.

Paris arrived at the holodeck just as Lt. Carey was completing his repairs. The engineer seemed amused.

"You know," he said, "most people aren't as eager as you are. You must have really missed this thing."

"With all my heart and soul," Paris told him.

Carey snorted. "Right." Then he replaced the panel on the bulkhead. "All yours, Lieutenant."

"Thanks. I'm forever in your debt."

"Goes without saying," the engineer replied good-naturedly. Then he gathered his tools and walked away.

Paris approached the interlocking holodeck doors and said, "Institute program Torres Alpha Omicron."

The doors opened, revealing a dank, fog-laden cavern. Torches were stuffed into crevices at intervals, creating enough light for him to see where he was going. But the place needed something more.

"Let's see," Paris said. "How about some candles—the long, twisted kind? And a little more of a breeze?"

At his command, the place filled with clusters of twisted candles. Their flames wavered and smoked in the mildew-ridden breeze.

"Better," he decided.

Paris looked around. What else? The sound of *krad'dak* drums? *Abin'do* pipes? A chorus singing Klingon war songs?

That might be a little *too* much, he told himself.

But certainly, there had to be an interrogator. Visualizing the figure he had come up with—not *Fek'lhr,* in the end, but merely a large and imposing warrior—the flight controller described the character to the computer.

A moment later, the interrogator appeared. He was big, all right, and meaner looking than Paris had envisioned. But that was all right. B'Elanna wouldn't think much of him if he wasn't mean-looking.

"And give him some assistants," Paris said.

Instantly, a half-dozen warriors appeared behind the interrogator. Somehow, that seemed like too many.

"Make it just two of them," he ordered.

The computer was quick to respond. All the assistants except two disappeared.

It went on like that for some time. Little by little, Paris added to the program, drawing on his research into Klingon traditions to devise the interrogator's behavior and speech patterns.

Finally, he was done. Looking around the cavern, he nodded. "Pretty good," he announced, "even if I do say so myself."

But the real test would come when B'Elanna arrived.

CHAPTER
2

PARIS MADE SURE HE WAS WAITING OUTSIDE ENGINEERING a couple of minutes before B'Elanna's shift was over. He just couldn't wait to show her what he'd come up with.

As the doors to engineering parted and she emerged into the corridor, she was surprised to see him. Pleasantly, the flight controller hoped, though he couldn't be entirely sure. After all, B'Elanna had that enigmatic half-frown, half-smile on her face.

"Fancy meeting you here," he said.

"Yes," B'Elanna replied, "fancy that."

"You'll never guess where I've been all day."

She looked at him. "I give up."

"In my quarters," Paris told her. "And then in the holodeck. But I think you'll agree that it was worth it."

B'Elanna sighed. "Don't tell me you were working on the Day of Honor program."

"I was working on the Day of Honor program." He held up his hand before she could respond. "Sorry. You asked me not to tell you that."

But his flip remark just covered his disappointment. Paris had come to know B'Elanna pretty well, and he could tell by her expression that she was having second thoughts about the program.

After he had worked so hard on it, too. But then, maybe he was reading too much into the look on her face.

"I'm having second thoughts about the program," B'Elanna told him.

Then again, maybe not.

"Why's that?" Paris asked.

The engineer shrugged. "I don't know. In retrospect, it seems a little . . . silly or something."

"Silly?" he echoed. "You wouldn't say that if you'd seen what I've done with it. There's nothing that's not downright solemn about this program—and I mean *nothing.*"

She considered him for a moment. "Tell you what, Tom. Let me sleep on it, okay?"

It wasn't as if Paris had a choice in the matter. "Sure. Whatever you say. I mean, it's up to you."

B'Elanna smiled. "Thanks." She patted him on the shoulder. "See you tomorrow."

Once again, he found himself standing there in a corridor as she made her getaway. Someday, he told himself, I'm going to find a way to make that woman a captive audience.

Yeah, right, he added—the day *targs* learn how to fly.

Kim picked up the three playing cards lying face down on the table and added them to the two already in his hand. Then he fanned the cards out in front of him, so he could see all five of them at a glance.

The two cards on the right were the jacks he had been dealt originally. Now, they had been joined by a deuce, a ten . . . and another jack. That gave Harry three of a kind—a pretty potent poker hand.

"All right," said Bandiero, the dark-haired man sitting across from him in *Voyager*'s echoing mess hall. He spoke without looking up from his cards. "Read 'em and weep."

Harry scanned the faces around the table. Bandiero, a lieutenant in astrophysics, was the one who had proposed the poker game in the first place. He, at least, might be a formidable opponent.

Ardan Trayl, a long-necked, green-skinned Mastikaan and a former Maquis, was new to the game. So were Neelix, the ship's Talaxian cook and unofficial morale officer, and Tuvok, its Vulcan security officer.

Or so they said.

Harry didn't expect much competition from Trayl or Neelix, at least until they learned how to play. But Tuvok was another question entirely. With his mastery of Vulcan logic, he had proven himself capable of some pretty amazing intellectual feats.

Of course, Tuvok wouldn't have a whole lot to go on, considering that all the cards in this game were dealt facedown. Theoretically, the only cards the Vulcan had seen were the eight that had passed through his hand.

Still, Harry wasn't about to underestimate Tuvok. He had seen people make that mistake in other situations and live to regret it.

Neelix, who was sitting next to the Vulcan, nudged Tuvok with his elbow. "Don't go reading my mind now, Mister Vulcan."

"You need not be concerned," Tuvok assured him, his voice free of resentment. "I cannot probe your thoughts unless I am in physical contact with you, Mr. Neelix. And even then, I would not do so without your permission."

"Kim bets," said Bandiero.

The ensign didn't want to chase anyone away. The idea was to reel the other players in slowly, getting them to increase their commitment each time, until, finally, they were too committed to turn back.

"Two replicator rations," he said. Removing two red chips from the stack in front of him, he added them to the pile in the center of the table.

Deep in contemplation of his cards, Neelix tapped his fingers on the table. Then he tapped them some more. And kept tapping them, much to the annoyance of everyone present.

"Neelix," Kim said at last.

The Talaxian looked up at him. "Yes?"

"We're waiting," the ensign reminded him.

"Ah," Neelix replied. "Sorry. I didn't mean to take so much time." Then he tapped his fingers some more.

"Neelix," said the astrophycisist.

"Hmmm?"

"We're not getting any younger."

The Talaxian glanced at him. "I'm just not sure

what to do." His eyes narrowing, he picked up ten chips, one after the other. Then he jiggled them in his hand.

"That's ten chips," Harry observed. "The maximum bet is five."

Neelix looked at him. "Is that true?"

"It is what we decided at the beginning of the game," Tuvok confirmed, skillfully containing whatever impatience he may have been experiencing.

The Talaxian took a breath, then slowly let it out. "I'm going to fold," he announced finally, then slapped his cards facedown on the table.

"You fold?" Bandiero echoed incredulously.

Neelix smiled at him. "It was either that or make a bet I didn't feel right about—if you know what I mean."

Bandiero shook his head. "No, as a matter of fact, I don't." He sighed and looked at Kim.

"Obviously," the ensign told Neelix, "you haven't quite mastered that part of the game. But we'll work on it. *Later.*" After all, Harry had three jacks and he was determined to make the most of them.

Bandiero turned to Tuvok. "It's up to you, sir."

The Vulcan frowned ever so slightly. "I, too, will fold. Of all the possible combinations of five playing cards, nearly fifty-two percent of them would be superior to the hand I hold. Therefore, it would be imprudent to place additional chips at risk."

"Now that," said Neelix, "is an interesting insight."

Tuvok glanced at him almost disdainfully. "I am glad you approve."

Harry bit his lip. There were only two other players left. Please, he thought, let *somebody* take the bait.

"It's my bet?" asked Trayl, his large black eyes turning in Bandiero's direction.

"That it is," Bandiero told him.

"Very well," said the Mastikaan. "I bet five chips." Separating them from his other chips with his long, slender fingers, he pushed five chips into the pot at the center of the table.

Inwardly, Harry smiled. Things were finally beginning to go his way.

Bandiero eyed Trayl the way a fisherman eyes a prize fish. "Tell you what. I'll see your five and raise you five."

Harry took another look at the astrophysicist's expression. It was completely deadpan—as emotionless as Tuvok's. There was no way of telling whether the man had a good hand or was bluffing.

Still, the ensign had the courage of his convictions. He didn't know what his opponents had, but he doubted they could beat three jacks.

"I'll see that bet," he said, taking chips out of his pile, "and bump it five more." He moved the chips into the center, then turned to the Mastikaan. "That's ten to you."

Trayl didn't so much as flinch. He simply moved the requisite number of chips into the pot.

Bandiero chuckled and tossed his cards on the table. "So much for my bluff. I'll let you two guys fight it out."

The Mastikaan regarded Harry with his big black orbs. "I believe I've beaten you." He placed his cards on the table, face up. "I have two pair—queens and fives. And all you have is three jacks."

"Two pair doesn't beat three jacks," said the ensign.

Suddenly, he realized something. "Wait a minute. I haven't shown you my cards yet. How did you know I had three jacks?"

Trayl blinked. "Simple," he replied. "I could see your cards reflected in your eyes."

Harry stared at the Mastikaan. "Ardan, you're not supposed to do that." He gestured to Tuvok. "That would be as bad as reading someone's mind."

The Mastikaan looked at him. "I wasn't cheating, Harry. Bandiero should have been more explicit when he explained the rules."

"I *was* explicit," Bandiero insisted. "Everybody knows you're not supposed to look at other people's cards. If you were, we would have played them all faceup."

Trayl frowned. "Obviously, not *everybody* knows it."

And before anyone could respond to his statement, he got up and left the mess hall. There was a moment of silence in his wake.

"Well," said the astrophysicist, "that went well."

Tuvok looked at him. "That leaves four of us, Mr. Bandiero. I believe it was you who said poker is most enjoyable with a minimum of five participants."

Bandiero shrugged. "Four can work, too."

"Listen," said Harry, "we can get someone else." He looked around the all-but-empty mess hall and tried to think of someone.

Tom had wanted to sit in. Unfortunately, he was on duty at the moment. So were the half-dozen others whose names occurred to the ensign on short notice.

He shook his head. He had heard of other ships with regularly scheduled poker games. Sometimes, several of them. Maybe it just took a while to get something like that started.

"I'm drawing a blank, too," Bandiero confessed. By then, he had begun gathering up the cards.

"How about Chell?" Neelix suggested. "He seems to be the gaming sort."

"Sure," said Harry, "when the game is *norr'tan,* or something else Bolians play. Chell already told us he wasn't interested."

Just then, the doors to the mess hall opened and two figures walked in. One was the Doctor—also known as the ship's Emergency Medical Hologram. The other was Seven of Nine.

Seven of Nine was a Borg.

Like everyone else on the ship, Harry knew she had once been a human. She had laughed, cried—done all the things humans do. But since her assimilation into the Borg collective as a child, she hadn't done any of those things.

It was creepy having her on *Voyager,* watching her walk the corridors, looking into those dead, cold eyes of hers. Still, the ensign reminded himself, there was something still alive in Seven of Nine. With a little luck, it could be brought to the surface again.

The Doctor seemed surprised to see Harry and the others sitting there. "Excuse me," he said. "I didn't think this facility would be in use."

"We are merely engaged in a game of poker," Tuvok explained. "If you require the use of the mess hall for something more important—"

"Not at all," the Doctor replied. "I was just show-ing Seven of Nine where the crew congregates to ingest foodstuffs. Pretty soon, she'll be doing the same thing."

"Oh?" said Bandiero, shuffling the cards in his hands.

"Yes," the Doctor replied. "I'm slowly weaning her off the energies she obtains from her cubicle and restoring her digestive system to full function. Mind you, it isn't a simple procedure—but if anyone can do it, I can."

Humility wasn't one of the Doctor's strongest qualities, Harry mused. But then, he didn't have a lot to be humble about. As an amalgam of the most gifted physicians in the Federation, he was the master of every medical technique and discipline known to man—and then some.

Suddenly, Harry had an idea. It was a little unorthodox, but he didn't want the poker game to die before it ever got started. Besides, he would be taking a step toward making an outsider an integral part of the crew.

"Say," the ensign said, "how'd you like to sit in? We could use another poker player."

The Doctor waved away the suggestion. "I'm no poker player, Mr. Kim. It's simply not part of my programming."

Harry smiled. "I could have guessed that, Doc. Actually, I was talking to Seven of Nine."

The Borg looked at him, evincing surprise—or anyway, a glitch in her otherwise detached behavior. "You wish me to take part in this . . ." She glanced at the deck of cards in Bandiero's hands. "What did you call it?"

"Poker," said the ensign. "It's a game of chance."

Seven of Nine tilted her head slightly. "And what is its purpose?"

Bandiero leaned closer to Harry. "You're barking up the wrong tree," he said. "Borg don't *play* cards. They *assimilate* them."

The ensign frowned at him. "That wasn't called for."

Bandiero didn't apologize. He just went back to shuffling the cards.

Harry turned to Seven of Nine again. "The purpose of poker—or any game—is to provide enjoyment. To take one's mind off one's work."

The Borg regarded him. "I have no work, Mr. Kim. And I do not believe I am capable of enjoyment."

"You see?" said Bandiero. "I told you you were wasting your time."

But the ensign wasn't ready to throw in the towel just yet. "You *might* be capable of enjoyment," he told Seven of Nine. "How do you know for sure until you've tried?"

"I know," said the Borg. And with that, she turned to the Doctor. "I believe you were going to show me the food preparation facilities."

The Doctor nodded. "Yes. Of course. Right this way," he said, gesturing to the cooking area.

Without waiting for him, Seven of Nine crossed the mess hall. In her wake, the Doctor turned back to Harry and shrugged. He seemed to be saying, "Even *my* manners are less reprehensible."

It was true, too. Compared to Seven of Nine, the Doctor had the social skills of a Federation ambassador.

Bandiero began doling out the cards. "The name of

the game is seven-card stud. Nothing's wild." He glanced at Harry. "Except some people's imaginations. I mean . . . a Borg rubbing elbows with real, live people? What's next? Tea with the Breen?"

Harry glared at him. "Shut up, Bandiero."

He glanced at Seven of Nine as she scrutinized Neelix's cooking equipment. She showed more interest in the pots and pans than she had in Kim or his fellow poker players.

"Just shut up," he added, for good measure.

As the Doctor escorted Seven of Nine out of the mess hall, he asked her if she had any questions. He expected that, if she did, they would concern the acquisition and digestion of foodstuffs.

For once, he was wrong.

"Ensign Kim mentioned work," she said.

The Doctor looked at her. "Yes, I believe he did."

"What work does he do?" the Borg asked.

The Doctor shrugged. "Mostly, he mans the ops station on the bridge. On occasion, however, he'll help out with some project. Why?"

"As members of the collective," said Seven of Nine, "we all had specific functions. After we performed them, there was a sense of accomplishment."

"I see," the Doctor responded. "And you would like to feel that sense of accomplishment again?"

The Borg blinked. "I would, yes."

"Well," said the Doctor, "I don't see why that couldn't be arranged. I mean, there always seems to be lots to do on the ship, and too few people to do it. I'm sure another set of hands would be quite welcome."

Seven of Nine turned to him. "Where would I work?"

"I don't know," the Doctor responded. "Where would you *like* to work?"

She didn't answer. However, the Doctor could tell she was giving the matter considerable thought.

"I'll tell you what," he said, realizing this was starting to fall outside the bounds of his expertise. "Why don't I take you to Commander Chakotay?"

"Why him?" the Borg asked.

"As first officer, he takes care of the duty assignments on the ship. You can discuss with him what type of thing you're looking for, and then he can tell you what's available."

Seven of Nine thought about it. Finally, she nodded. "Yes," she said. "That would be a good idea."

CHAPTER
3

As THE DOOR AHEAD OF HIM IRISED OPEN WITH A CREAKY complaint, Temmis Rahmin came out onto the bridge of his people's ship. The place was stark and dreary, the only light coming from the monitors that hung above a dozen consoles along the periphery.

Still, it was functional. He was grateful for that, at least.

Nodding to the technicians standing at the consoles, Rahmin assumed his customary position in the center of the bridge. In the process, he did his best to ignore the hunger gnawing at his insides like a cruel, infinitely patient predator. After all, his comrades were just as hungry as he was, and they weren't complaining.

Fortunately, Rahmin had gotten rather good at ignoring his discomforts in the last year or so. At this point, only his memories had the power to cause him any pain.

He raised his eyes to the hexagonal viewscreen that loomed in front of him. The image on the screen flickered and jumped and fell victim to waves of static, which had gotten worse over the last several months. But in between these inconveniences, the screen gave Rahmin an adequate picture of the stars flowing by his vessel.

In his younger days, when he was part of his people's great, forward-looking push to explore the universe, he had seen the stars flow by faster. But that was a different time, before those same stars rained doom on them—a doom from which they were still struggling to recover.

Yes, Rahmin thought, a *very* different time—when they could be proud of their creations, when they could depend on them.

The maximum velocity of *this* vessel was only ten times the speed of light. Rahmin sighed. At such a speed, interstellar travel took forever. He and his crew had left their home system behind an entire year ago, and since then they had encountered only one other system.

It had afforded them little in the way of supplies. They were hoping the next one would serve them better—that it would have planets similar enough to that of their birth to provide them with food and perhaps even medicinal herbs. But by their cartographer's estimate, it would be another month before they got there.

In a month, more of them would falter. And having

faltered, some would die. It was a hard fact of the life they had been forced to adopt.

Rahmin shook his head ruefully. If only their power sources hadn't diminished so quickly. If only they had had the materials and the expertise to keep their engines in good repair.

If, if, and if again. He was sick to death of *ifs*.

"Rahmin!" someone called out.

He turned and saw one of his technicians beckoning to him. Curious, Rahmin crossed the bridge to stand by the man's side.

"What is it?" he asked.

The technician, a fellow named Aruun, pointed to his monitor, which hung from the bulkhead at eye level. Following the gesture, Rahmin inspected the monitor's blue-on-black grid.

"I don't see—" he began.

Then he *did* see. In the corner of the screen, there was a tiny red blip—so tiny, in fact, he would have missed it if he hadn't been looking for it.

"A ship," he breathed.

"A ship," Aruun confirmed. "And it is not one of ours."

It was the first alien vessel they had spotted since they left the world of their birth. Rahmin swallowed. This was an important occasion—and it would require him to make an equally important decision.

He turned to Aruun. "Have you been able to gauge their speed?"

The man nodded. "They're traveling at twenty times the speed of light. If we were behind them, we would have no chance of catching up. However, our courses seem to be converging."

"So we can intercept them," Rahmin concluded.

"We can indeed," Aruun assured him.

Rahmin considered the information. By then, a crowd of technicians had begun to gather about them. Only those in charge of the piloting mechanism and life support had remained at their posts.

"Did I hear correctly?" asked a woman named Yshaarta. "Have we sighted an alien ship?"

"Yes," said Aruun. "And we can make contact with it." He turned to Rahmin, containing his excitement in deference to his superior. "That is, if Rahmin thinks it's a good idea."

Everyone looked at Rahmin. He frowned under their scrutiny. He had never expressed a desire for this kind of responsibility. But then, that was not the only burden he hadn't asked for.

"So?" asked a man named Tarrig. "What *do* you think, Rahmin?"

Rahmin took a breath, then let it out. If they established contact with the aliens, one of three things would happen. They would benefit from the association, emerge from it much as they were now . . . or be damaged, perhaps even destroyed.

On the other hand, he thought, their situation was a bad one—and it was getting worse each day. If there was ever a time to take a chance, this appeared to be that time.

Rahmin turned to their pilot, who like everyone else was looking at him. "Set a course to intercept," he commanded.

The pilot smiled and obeyed. And Rahmin hoped to heaven that his choice had been the right one.

* * *

B'Elanna was dreaming. In her dream, she was in a lecture hall at Starfleet Academy. But none of her classmates were there—only B'Elanna herself and her warp-physics instructor, Benton Horvath.

Horvath was tops in his field. B'Elanna respected him for that. Time and again, she had done her best to impress the man. But somehow, despite all her preparation, all her love for the subject, she had fallen short.

The professor's back was to her as he made some calculations on a data padd. His bald spot caught the light. Suddenly, he spoke up.

"I asked you a question, cadet."

B'Elanna knew he could only mean her. But she hadn't heard any question. Or, at least, she didn't *remember* hearing one.

"I'm sorry," she said. "Could you repeat it?"

Horvath cast a glance at her over his shoulder. A *withering* glance.

"All right, Mr. Torres. Once again, and this time I'll try to make it a bit more memorable." He cleared his throat. "Is that all right?"

B'Elanna nodded. "Yes, fine. I mean, thank you."

Horvath turned back to his padd. "All right. You're proceeding at warp 1. No remarkable engine inefficiencies, no unusual subspace hindrances. All is going according to plan. Got it?"

"Yes," said B'Elanna.

"Well, don't pat yourself on the back just yet, Mr. Torres. Back on this ship of ours, a problem arises. Something rips off one of our two nacelles. I don't care what it is, frankly—a subspace anomaly or what-have-you. The point is, the damnable thing is wrenched away. Still with me?"

"So far," she assured him.

"The question," said Horvath, "is what do you do?"

B'Elanna looked at him—or rather, at his back. "Do?" she echoed. "I mean . . . what can I *possibly* do?"

The instructor turned to her. "I asked you first. Come on, Mr. Torres. This isn't so difficult."

She shook her head. "If a nacelle falls off, different parts of the vessel end up travelling at different speeds. The ship is torn apart. There's nothing *anyone* can do about it."

Horvath smiled a wicked smile. "Isn't there? Think, Mr. Torres."

B'Elanna found her mouth was dry all of a sudden. She licked her lips. "I . . . I don't know," she whispered.

The instructor looked disgusted. "Come on," he said, his voice like a lash. "People are depending on you, Mr. Torres. Your captain is depending on you. If you can't help them, they'll all die."

The cadet grabbed her head with both hands. It was insane. Snippets of warp-field engineering lore flitted crazily through her brain, as elusive as black butterflies on Kessik IV, where she grew up.

Field formation is controllable in a fore-to-aft direction. The cumulative field-layer forces reduce the apparent mass of the vehicle and impart the required velocities. During saucer separation . . .

"The interactive warp-field controller software," B'Elanna blurted. "It alters the field geometry—"

"No!" Horvath barked. "It doesn't react quickly enough." He shook his head disdainfully. "The deck-plates are shivering, Mr. Torres. The stress is unimaginable. Do something! Do it now!"

"It's impossible!" she growled. "There's nothing a person can do!"

His eyes narrowed. "You're telling me it's impossible?"

"Yes," B'Elanna grated between clenched teeth. "Impossible!"

Horvath's mouth twisted. "You'll never be an engineer in *this* fleet with an attitude like that! You're a quitter, Mr. Torres! A quitter!"

"No!" she screamed. "No! N—"

Suddenly, B'Elanna found herself in her bedroom. She was sitting upright in the darkness, covered in cold sweat, her heart banging against her ribs so hard it hurt.

It was a dream. Only a dream, for godsakes. And, she told herself, you were absolutely right. There's nothing you can do if a nacelle tears off—except try to make your last thought a happy one.

Benton Horvath was a bastard, but he would never have asked her a question like that. Not in real life. Only in an irritating, soul-scouring gut-wrencher of a dream.

B'Elanna took a breath and let it out. Suddenly, a strange feeling crept up on her—a feeling that she had forgotten something important.

"Computer," she asked, "what time is it?"

"It's seven forty-five a.m.," the computer told her.

B'Elanna cursed beneath her breath. Seven forty-five? She was due to conduct a fuel-cell overhaul in engineering in fifteen minutes. How would it look if the chief engineer was late for something like that?

Somehow, she realized, she had forgotten to give the computer a wake-up command. But how? She *always* gave the computer a wake-up command. Of all nights to slip up, she thought.

Then B'Elanna remembered. It was the Day of Honor.

No, she thought. Don't say it. Don't even think it. You've shaken your Day of Honor luck.

From now on, she reminded herself, only *good* things are going to happen on this day. You'll see, she insisted. Only good things.

Except, apparently, bad dreams. And forgotten wake-up calls.

Putting both those things out of her mind, B'Elanna tossed her covers aside, swung her legs out of bed, and padded into the bathroom, where she manipulated the controls on the side of the sonic shower stall. When she heard the emitter heads begin to hum, she stepped inside.

If she hurried, B'Elanna told herself, she could still make the cell overhaul. A minute in the shower, another minute to pull on her uniform, and maybe three more minutes for breakfast. That would leave her as many as ten minutes to reach engineering.

It could happen. It *would* happen.

B'Elanna had built up her resolve to a fever pitch when she heard the emitter heads sputter. Huh, she thought. That's strange. Suddenly, they let out a shriek so loud and so grating she thought her eardrums would burst.

"Damn!" she yelped, leaping out of the shower stall.

The emitter heads continued to shriek, undaunted by the glare B'Elanna was leveling at them. All over the galaxy, she imagined, animals were hearing the sound and going nuts.

So was she—but for an entirely different reason. After all, she was standing in the middle of the bathroom without her clothes, no cleaner than she had been a minute ago.

Worse, B'Elanna couldn't let the shower keep screeching like that. Aside from the discomfort it would cause her neighbors, the mechanism could build up a feedback loop. Then every EPS relay in the corridor would have to be reset—or, if luck went against them, replaced.

The Klingon in her wanted to rip the shower out of the wall. Fortunately, that Klingon had human company.

Still naked, teeth grating against the noise, B'Elanna knelt and removed the cover from the relay next to the shower. It wasn't a difficult task, but it *was* one that couldn't be rushed.

Then, without benefit of the tools one usually used for something like this, she cut off power to the shower unit. As suddenly as it had begun, the shrieking stopped.

It was quiet in the bathroom. Unnaturally quiet— except for the ringing in B'Elanna's ears.

Unfortunately, she had used up not only her shower time, but her breakfast time as well. And unless she got a move on, she wouldn't have time to get dressed either. Muttering beneath her breath, she went back into her bedroom and opened the door to her closet.

Picking out one of the uniforms she found hanging there, she pulled it on as quickly as she could. Then she bolted for the door, unnerved, unshowered, and unfed.

And even with all that, there was no guarantee she would make it to engineering in time.

CHAPTER
4

CHAKOTAY FOUND SEVEN OF NINE STANDING IN HER Borg cubicle. It chilled him a little every time he saw the thing, in that it was a remnant of the ship's transformation.

As the first officer approached the cubicle, Seven of Nine noticed him and stepped down. "Commander Chakotay," she said.

"I understand you wanted to see me."

"I am told you are the officer in charge of personnel," said the Borg. "That you prepare the 'duty assignments.' Is that the correct phrase?"

"That's right," he replied.

But inside, he was wondering why Seven of Nine was suddenly interested in duty assignments. Unless . . .

The Borg blinked. "I'm finding it difficult to spend

so much time alone," she said. "I'm unaccustomed to it. The hours don't pass quickly."

Chakotay couldn't help but sympathize. He knew how great a loss it had been for Seven of Nine when she was disconnected from the Borg collective.

"Also," she said, "I had a sense of accomplishment among the Borg. I wish to experience that sense again."

"I can understand that," Chakotay said. "How can we help?"

But even before the Borg opened her mouth, he had an idea what her answer would be.

"I have been considering the matter carefully," Seven of Nine told him. "I would like to request a duty assignment."

It was just what the first officer had expected. He mulled over the ramifications before he spoke again.

"Did you have something specific in mind?" he asked.

The Borg blinked. "Yes."

Then she told Chakotay what it was.

He sighed. Why couldn't she have asked to help Neelix in the mess hall? Or to take a shift in astrophysics?

"I'll see what I can do," he told Seven of Nine.

The corridor outside the turbolift was empty except for B'Elanna. Abandoning any pretense of decorum, she sprinted down the hall as if the devil and all his demons were after her.

That is, she thought wildly, the devil of my father's people. Klingons didn't really have such a thing.

As B'Elanna approached the doors to engineering, she had to decelerate to give the metal panels time to slide aside for her. Naturally, they did this with the most agonizing slowness. Then, with what she estimated as seconds to spare, the lieutenant burst into engineering.

As she stood there, illuminated by the brightly pulsating warp core, she wondered where everyone was. Instead of the four engineers she had expected to see, only two were present—Carey and Vorik. Both of them were sitting at consoles, performing diagnostics in accordance with standing orders.

Carey looked up at her. "Ah. Morning, Lieutenant." After a moment, his brow furrowed. "Say . . . are you all right?"

"Fine." B'Elanna breathed. "Why?"

The redheaded man shrugged. "You seem to be perspiring. I thought it might be a symptom."

She returned his stare. "A symptom of what, Mr. Carey?"

He shrugged again. "You know, the thing that's got Nicoletti and Chafin under the weather." Suddenly, understanding dawned. "Wait a minute. You don't know about Nicoletti and Chafin, do you?"

B'Elanna shook her head. "No."

"They are ill," Vorik interjected. He swiveled his chair around to face his superior. "The Doctor informed us a moment ago."

Annoyed, B'Elanna tapped her commbadge. "Torres to sickbay. Are you there, Doctor?"

"Indeed," came the response from the ship's "physician"—actually, a holographic manifestation of the Emergency Medical Program. "If you're concerned about Nicoletti and Chafin, don't be. They have a simple virus, for which I possess a simple cure. In four or five hours, they should be as good as new."

"In four or five hours," B'Elanna echoed.

"That's correct," said the Doctor. "Now, if there's nothing else, Lieutenant, I'll finish up with my patients."

"Go ahead," said the chief engineer. She turned to Vorik, then Carey, and realized she'd acted like a complete madwoman for nothing. "I suppose it's silly to overhaul the fuel cells when half the shift is absent."

"It would seem so," Vorik agreed.

B'Elanna sighed. "Let's do it tomorrow, then. I'll notify Nicoletti and Chafin. And while I'm at it, I'll remind them that I'm to be notified *personally* whenever they're sick."

"Whatever you say," Carey told her.

Abruptly, a throaty yet eminently feminine voice cut into their conversation. "Janeway to Lieutenant Torres."

B'Elanna looked up at the intercom grid hidden in the ceiling. "Torres here. What can I do for you, Captain?"

"Harry's having some trouble with his console," Janeway told her. "Can you send someone up here to take a look at it?"

"Right away," the chief engineer replied.

"Thanks," said the captain. "Janeway out."

"I've fixed that console before," Carey noted. "I think I know what might be wrong with it."

B'Elanna nodded. "Go to it."

In one motion, Carey got up and headed for the exit. A moment later, he was gone, on his way to the bridge.

She turned to Vorik. "How are the diagnostics going?"

"I have not detected any problems or anomalies," the Vulcan responded. "All systems appear to be functioning within acceptable parameters."

B'Elanna nodded. "Good." Maybe this day would turn out to be a decent one after all, despite its hectic start.

She had barely completed the thought when she heard something pop. Before she could turn to find the origin of the sound, she heard another one—a high-pitched hissing.

Then B'Elanna saw the reason for it. A conduit was leaking plasma coolant. The gas was coming out in a sizzling, white jet.

She glanced at Vorik. The Vulcan was working at his console, trying to determine what had happened.

"Now what?" B'Elanna asked.

Vorik turned to her, chagrined. "It seems there has been a rupture in the coolant injector."

"I can see that," she told him. Why haven't you sealed it off?"

"I am attempting to do so," he replied.

But he wasn't having much luck. B'Elanna darted to the nearest workstation to see why.

In the second or two it took her to get there, the problem got worse—a lot worse. By the time she brought up the coolant system on her screen, the tiny stream of gas had turned into a geyser.

So much for diagnostics, B'Elanna thought bitterly.

If this went on, engineering would become uninhabitable. Worse, a whole range of operating systems would be compromised.

Ergo, it *couldn't* go on. B'Elanna held on to that thought as she worked furiously at her console. Unfortunately, though she had pinpointed the leak, she couldn't seem to stop it any better than the Vulcan could.

Then she realized why. There was a point farther up the line where coolant pressure had built past the breaking point. If she was going to stop the leak, she would have to take care of the pressure problem first.

"I am having difficulty identifying the cause of the leak," Vorik reported. He was bent over his monitor, eyes narrowed with concentration.

"So am I," she told him.

Suddenly, B'Elanna's workstation seized up. As she had feared, the leak was starting to affect other systems in the vicinity.

Cursing beneath her breath, she tried another workstation—and got the same results. In other words, nothing. And though she tried not to breathe in the coolant, it was already starting to make her head throb.

B'Elanna checked out a third workstation and a fourth before she found one that was still functioning. This time, she didn't try to locate the problem—she just reacted to it. If she cut off every possible source of the gas, she would eventually stem the tide.

At least, that was her strategy. Desperately, she ran her strong, slender fingers over her padd, shutting down access point after access point. All around engineering, conduits were closing up, containing the gas that flowed through them.

But it didn't seem to be working. The leak wasn't abating—and B'Elanna was swiftly running out of possibilities.

She bit her lip. Think, she told herself. Where else can this damned gas be coming from?

The EPS manifold? It seemed unlikely, but . . .

"Try shutting off the EPS manifold," she called over the hiss of the escaping coolant. "Maybe that'll help."

Vorik did as she suggested. It didn't diminish the stream of coolant one iota. "The EPS manifold is not the problem," the Vulcan told her.

"I don't get it," B'Elanna rasped.

Vorik looked at her, his brow wrinkling ever so slightly. "Is it possible the pressure is coming from . . . the field coils?"

She considered the possibility. "No," she decided finally. "But let's give it a try anyway."

Vorik tapped out a command on his console—then shook his head. Obviously, thought B'Elanna, the thing had stopped working.

She tried the same thing at her own station. Nothing happened. Pounding on it savagely, she watched the Vulcan dart across engineering and plant himself at another station.

Let this one work, B'Elanna pleaded inwardly.

It *did*.

Vorik worked with a sense of urgency B'Elanna had seldom seen in a being of any species. A moment later, the stream of plasma coolant began to decrease noticeably in volume.

"That's better," B'Elanna cried out. "Close it down completely."

Vorik worked some more. The jet of escaping gas diminished by degrees, until it stopped altogether. Silence reigned in engineering, punctuated only by the subtle throbbing of the warp core.

B'Elanna took a deep breath. Another crisis averted, she thought. She glanced at Vorik, who was still standing over his console.

"Good work, Ensign."

The Vulcan met her gaze. "Perhaps it would be advisable to reconfigure the coolant assembly. That would give us greater control over pressure valve emissions in the future."

B'Elanna felt herself sagging a little. "Vorik," she said, "you're probably right. And tomorrow we can do it first thing. But not today."

The Vulcan looked puzzled. She didn't blame him.

"I do not understand," he said. "Why wait until tomorrow when it would be to our advantage to start—"

"Not today," B'Elanna barked, surprising even herself with the ferocity in her voice.

Vorik lifted an eyebrow at her vehemence. But wisely, he didn't question her judgment.

"As you wish," he replied.

Then he turned and moved toward a more distant workstation. B'Elanna watched him go, more than a little angry with herself. Vorik had deserved better from his superior officer—especially after he'd come through for her in the clutch.

But before she could go after the Vulcan, she saw Tom enter engineering. He had a padd in his hands.

And he was more cheerful than usual, though the reason for it wasn't readily apparent.

"Good morning," he said. "Here's the conn evaluation you wanted."

B'Elanna regarded him. "Thanks."

Tom took note of her sullen mood. Sensing something was awry, he looked around and noted the hole in the coolant conduit. Then he sniffed the ozone in the air. His nose wrinkled.

"Something happen in here?" he inquired.

"Don't ask," she told him.

Tom chuckled. "But—"

"I said don't ask."

The flight controller regarded her for a moment. When he spoke again, it was with a bit more care. "We still on for dinner tonight?"

B'Elanna frowned and looked away. "I don't know. I may have to work." She shrugged. "I'll let you know."

Tom nodded. "Okay . . ." He hesitated, obviously not sure whether to raise the next subject or not. "And have you decided if you're, uh, going through with it? The Day of Honor program, I mean?"

She turned on him. "I have—and I'm not. This has started out to be a lousy day and the last thing I need is to get involved with some obscure Klingon ritual. Okay?"

He held his hand up as if in self-defense. "Hey, it's all the same to me. You were the one who suggested it."

"I know," the engineer said. "And for one sentimental minute, I thought I might go through with it. But not anymore."

Tom cracked a smile. "Of course not. Wouldn't want to get too sentimental, would we?"

B'Elanna realized that she was being unfair with him—just as she had been unfair with Vorik a moment earlier.

"Look, she said, "it hasn't exactly been the most pleasant morning of my life. First, I overslept because I forgot to tell the computer to wake me. Then the acoustic inverter in my sonic shower blew out."

Tom cringed. "That'll make your hair stand on end."

"So I didn't have time for breakfast," B'Elanna went on. "And when I got here, two people were out sick and I had to cancel the fuel-cell overhaul, and then an injector burst for no reason at all and started spewing plasma coolant over everything."

Tom grunted. "That's a run of bad luck, all right."

"So I'm in a bad mood," she told him. "And I know I'm being a little testy, and I apologize in advance . . . but I'm not very good company right now."

He didn't try to talk her out of her mood. He just smiled affably and headed for the door.

"It's okay," Tom said. "Think about that dinner . . ."

But he looked back at her for a moment. And when he did, their eyes locked, and B'Elanna found herself grateful for his understanding.

"Thanks," she said.

"It's okay," Tom assured her. "I've had bad days, too."

With that, he left her. But as he walked out of engineering, Commander Chakotay walked in.

"Morning, Commander," said Tom.

Chakotay nodded to him. "Lieutenant."

Then, in a voice just loud enough for B'Elanna to hear, the flight controller said, "Be careful."

The first officer glanced at him as he passed.

Crossing engineering, Chakotay approached B'Elanna.

Abruptly, the first officer's nose scrunched up. He looked around—and his gaze fell on the damaged conduit. Then he turned back to B'Elanna.

"Something happen in here?"

"It's under control," she told him.

Chakotay's eyes went hard for a moment. When he asked a question, he liked it answered—accurately and completely. B'Elanna knew that. After all, she was serving under him before either of them had heard of *Voyager*.

But over the years, the first officer had gotten used to B'Elanna's flares of temper. He had come to understand her. And at that moment, he obviously realized all was not well with her.

Instead of taking umbrage at her response, he smiled. "That's good," he said. "I'm glad."

B'Elanna sighed. "You came here for a reason, I imagine."

Chakotay shrugged. "What makes you think I haven't stopped by just to say hello?"

The engineer was in no mood for games. She was about to say so, but thought better of it. Instead, she bent over a workstation and checked to see if it was functional again.

Another executive officer might have interpreted

that as insubordination. Chakotay knew her better than that.

"Actually," he conceded, "you're right. I came to tell you that something interesting just happened."

"And what's that?" the engineer asked absently.

"Seven of Nine requested a duty assignment."

"Fascinating," B'Elanna responded.

"You don't know the half of it," the commander told her. "She wants to work in engineering."

B'Elanna whirled to face the first officer. In her fury, "What?" was all she could get out.

"As you know," he said reasonably, "the Borg use transwarp conduits to travel through space faster than warp speed. If we could create one of these conduits for our *own* use—"

"We don't know anything about transwarp technology," B'Elanna snapped. "Playing around with it could be dangerous."

"That's where Seven of Nine comes in," Chakotay countered. "She's offered to work with you. To make sure nothing goes wrong."

"And you *believe* her?" the engineer asked. "She's a Borg. Who knows what her real motives might be?"

"As a matter of fact," the commander said, "I *do* believe her. She's having a tough time making the transition from the collective. She wants something to occupy her mind. Something to make her feel useful."

B'Elanna flashed him a scornful look. "I never thought of you as naive, Chakotay. The Delta Quadrant has turned you soft." She bit her lip. "The bottom line is I don't want her working here in engineering."

The commander's expression hardened again. His

eyes became chips of obsidian. "The bottom line," he told her, "is I'm giving you an order and you're going to follow it . . . *Lieutenant.*"

They glared at each other for a moment, neither of them eager to give ground. B'Elanna wanted to rage at Chakotay, but she held her emotions in check—because, patient as he was, even *he* had his limits.

Finally, she replied, "Whatever you say, sir."

The commander didn't seem altogether satisfied with that response—but he accepted it. Turning, he left engineering.

B'Elanna looked after him, angry and resentful. She had been in a bad mood before Chakotay arrived. Now, it was positively foul.

Returning her attention to her workstation, she assessed the damage to operating protocols caused by the coolant leak. Then, her jaw clenched, she set about repairing it.

CHAPTER

5

JANEWAY WAS SITTING BEHIND THE DESK IN HER READY room, going over supply reports, when she heard a chime.

"Come in," she said.

As the doors slid aside, they revealed her first officer. Chakotay wasn't smiling as he entered.

Not a good sign, the captain thought. But then, she hadn't expected Chakotay to come back from engineering with a grin on his face. Pushing back her chair and getting to her feet, she gestured to the window seat in front of her observation port.

Her exec accepted the seat. A moment later, Janeway came around her desk and sat beside him.

"Not the easiest thing you've ever had to tell her?" the captain asked.

Chakotay grunted softly. "B'Elanna wasn't happy about the idea."

"But she'll get over it," the captain suggested.

He nodded. "Yes, she will."

Janeway stood again, stretching out the kinks in her neck. "Unfortunately, B'Elanna isn't the only member of the crew who's uncomfortable with the idea of a Borg on the ship."

Chakotay frowned. "I'm afraid Seven of Nine doesn't help her own case. She tends to put people off because she's so direct. So—"

"Honest," said the captain.

The commander nodded again. "That's one word for it."

Janeway smiled sympathetically. "I know. That's what I like about her. Her directness. Her honesty."

"But," Chakotay pointed out, "she still doesn't have any real perspective on what it is to be human."

"And that's the challenge," the captain replied, warming to the subject. "To help ease her back into humanity."

Chakotay smiled. "To make her comfortable among us."

"Exactly. That's the only way she'll be able to rejoin the world she was born into. The human world. I think it's a good sign that she wants a duty assignment. She's taking a step toward us."

Her exec grunted. "No argument there."

Janeway thought for a moment. "I need to speak with Seven of Nine. Give her the lay of the land, as it were. After all, in the collective, no one person was in charge. She's never encountered a chain of command before."

"I'll tell her you want to speak with her," said Chakotay.

The captain nodded. "Please do."

Tuvok glanced at his tactical board, where one of the monitors showed that there had been a release of plasma coolant in engineering. Since neither Captain Janeway nor Commander Chakotay was on the bridge, the Vulcan contacted the individual in charge of that section directly.

"Tuvok to Lieutenant Torres. Please respond."

There was silence for a moment. Then Torres said, "I'm here, Tuvok. And if you're going to ask me about the coolant release . . . *don't.* It's over, all right? Let's leave it at that."

With that, she terminated the intraship communication. The Vulcan cocked an eyebrow. Such a reply was unusual, even for such a volatile personality as the chief engineer's.

What was *not* unusual was the incident Torres had described as "over." As *Voyager's* tactical officer, Tuvok had gotten used to the occurrence of minor systems dysfunctions. In fact, he had come to expect them.

After all, *Voyager* wasn't like other starships. She wasn't able to put into drydock for an overhaul every so often, the nearest starbase being decades away at high warp.

As a result, the ship and her crew were forced to face each problem as it arose, and handle it as best they could. In most cases, that meant a considerable amount of improvisation.

It was a tribute to the ingenuity and dedication of Captain Janeway and her operations staff that they had met each new challenge and surmounted it. In fact, it stirred a certain amount of pride in Tuvok to be associated with such capable people.

Not that he would ever tell them that to their faces. He was a Vulcan, and his species didn't indulge in displays of emotion.

Returning his attention to his monitors, Tuvok initiated a long-range scan. After all, it was the lieutenant's job to scan for external occurrences as well as internal ones.

As Seven of Nine entered the captain's ready room, Janeway turned away from her observation port. "Thank you for coming," she said.

The Borg didn't answer. She just stood there in the center of the room, awaiting the captain's next remark.

"I understand you want to work in engineering," Janeway noted.

"That's correct," Seven of Nine replied.

"Engineering is a sensitive area."

The Borg looked at her. "Sensitive?"

"Important," the captain explained, "in the sense that a . . . mistake there could cause a great deal of damage."

Seven of Nine blinked. "I can see how that would be so."

Janeway decided to quit beating around the bush. "You told me you wouldn't make any more attempts to contact the Borg . . . and, of course, I want to believe that's true."

"I assure you it is," said Seven of Nine.

The captain regarded her. Janeway's instincts told her the Borg was on the level, and her instincts were usually right.

"I've decided not to post a security detail while you're in engineering, Seven of Nine. But you have to realize, there are rules. You'll be expected to follow our protocols."

The Borg nodded. "I will do so."

Janeway believed she would, too. "You'll report directly to Lieutenant Torres and obey any order she gives you."

"I understand," said Seven of Nine.

The captain shifted gears. "One more thing. Your 'designation'—Seven of Nine. It's a little cumbersome. Wouldn't you prefer to be called by your given name, Annika?"

The Borg seemed vaguely troubled by the prospect—as if she felt things were moving a little too fast. "I have been Seven of Nine for as long as I can remember," she responded.

Mindful that too much change could be threatening, Janeway looked for a compromise. "All right. But maybe we could streamline it a little. How would you feel about . . . Seven?"

The Borg considered it. "Imprecise," she decided. "But acceptable."

Abruptly, a familiar voice filled the room. "Tuvok to Captain Janeway."

"I'm here," the captain answered.

"Please come to the bridge," the Vulcan requested in his clipped, efficient tone. "A ship is approaching."

Janeway looked at Seven of Nine. The Borg looked back.

Curious, the captain led the way out onto *Voyager*'s small but efficient bridge, where Chakotay was waiting for her. Janeway's eyes were drawn instinctively to the forward viewscreen.

She saw the image of a small alien ship there. Clearly, the vessel had seen better days. Its exterior hull looked worn in spots, and some of the devices that projected from it were slightly bent.

The captain turned to Tuvok, seeking whatever information he could provide. "Report," she said.

"The vessel is damaged but still functional," the Vulcan informed her, intent on his readouts. "Energy emissions are so low it probably isn't capable of warp speed. However, sensors show several dozen lifesigns aboard." He paused. "We're being hailed, Captain."

"Open a channel," she told him.

Tuvok complied. A moment later, the face of a wizened, thin, and sickly being appeared on the screen.

The being's skin was a pale green, his eyes a deeper shade of the same color—though they lacked luster. His only other remarkable feature was the hard-looking ridge that ran back from the bridge of his nose through the middle of his scalp.

His ship's interior seemed stark, devoid of any and all amenities. Energy seemed to be in short supply as well, if the lights flickering behind him were any indication.

Janeway lifted her chin. "I'm Captain Kathryn Janeway of the Federation starship *Voyager.*"

The being on the viewscreen nodded. "I am Rahmin. My people are the Caatati." He glanced at his surroundings. "I apologize for our appearance, and for the condition of our ship. We were assimilated by the Borg over a year ago. We lost . . . everything."

Everything, the captain thought. There was a world of pain in the word. It seemed the devastation created by the Borg was everywhere.

Reminded of Seven of Nine, she glanced over her shoulder. The Borg was standing off to the side, where Rahmin couldn't see her. Just as well, Janeway thought, as she turned back to the Caatati.

"How many of you escaped?" she asked.

Rahmin sighed. "A few thousand, on thirty ships. All that's left from a planet of millions."

Chakotay winced. The captain, too, felt a pang of empathy for these people. "I'm sorry," she said earnestly.

Rahmin seemed uncomfortable with the response. He shifted his weight from one foot to the other.

"Captain," he replied, "I want to assure you of something. My people were once proud and accomplished. Before the Borg came, we had enjoyed peace for centuries. We pursued scientific inquiry . . . produced art and literature." He shook his head. "We weren't always in such reduced circumstances."

Janeway nodded. "I understand."

"It pains me to have to ask this," Rahmin said. "But I have eighty-eight people to care for on this vessel. If we are to survive much longer, we need food . . . medicines. Is there any way you could help us?"

Clearly, Rahmin was a proud man, and it was difficult for him to make the request. Janeway didn't want to make it any harder on him.

"Of course," she told the alien. "Send us a list of your needs and we'll see what we can do."

Rahmin smiled at the captain, though his expression was only a faint echo of her own. "I'm deeply grateful," he said. "If it's not too much to ask . . . is there any way you might also spare a small quantity of thorium isotopes? Without it, our systems can't function."

"I think we can arrange that," Janeway responded. "I'll speak to my chief engineer, B'Elanna Torres."

Rahmin looked as if a weight had been lifted from him. "You can't imagine what this means to us, Captain. Thank you."

And with that, his image blinked out, giving way to that of his vessel.

Janeway looked to the intercom grid in the ceiling. "Bridge to engineering," she said.

B'Elanna was working at a console in engineering, making sure there were no further pressure buildups in the coolant lines, when she noticed a flashing symbol in the corner of her screen. It was a sign that sensor information or other important data was being relayed to her by a bridge officer.

Tapping her keyboard, she accepted the data. An image showed up on her monitor—that of a thin, sickly-looking alien in a dim, almost featureless environment. He was in the middle of a sentence.

". . . assimilated by the Borg over a year ago," the alien related, his voice taut with pain. "We lost everything."

B'Elanna heard the captain ask for details, and she heard the alien supply them. But she was no longer looking at her monitor—not really. The engineer was thinking about Seven of Nine.

After all, that Borg may have been on the vessel that attacked the alien's people. She may have aided in the devastation of the alien's homeworld. And if she hadn't, she had no doubt done the same thing elsewhere.

Seven of Nine was a Borg, a cold-blooded killer. How was it so easy for people to forget that?

Focusing on her monitor again, B'Elanna followed the rest of the captain's conversation with the alien. She learned what kind of race the Borg had assimilated and nearly destroyed—a proud and accomplished one.

"It pains me to have to ask this," the alien said, "but I have eighty-eight people to care for. If we are to survive much longer, we need food . . . medicines. Is there any way you could help us?"

Janeway assured him that she would do so. Then the alien made another request—this time, for thorium isotopes. The captain said she would have to speak to her chief engineer first.

The alien thanked her. A moment later, his image vanished, replaced by a view of his ship. B'Elanna shuddered at the sight of it. It was a wonder it still functioned.

Then, as she had expected, she received a call from Janeway on the intercom. "Bridge to engineering."

B'Elanna looked up at the ceiling. "Torres here." And to save time: "I'm aware of what's going on, Captain."

"Good," said Janeway. "Then you know I'd like to help the Caatati in any way we can. Can you and your people come up with the isotopes Rahmin requested?"

B'Elanna thought for a moment. "It might take us a while to modify the intermix ratio to produce thorium, but we should be able to work it out."

"Keep me informed," the captain told her.

B'Elanna assured her that she would do that. Then, glad for the chance to do something productive before the day was over, she got to work.

CHAPTER
6

JANEWAY SAT AT THE HEAD OF THE TABLE IN *VOYAGER*'S briefing room and watched Rahmin stare at the unblinking stars. The Caatati's expression was a decidedly wistful one.

"They seem so much friendlier here," he remarked.

"The stars?" she asked.

Rahmin nodded, his eyes glinting with reflections of their light. "I'd forgotten how beautiful they can be. The last year or so, they've been my enemies—always dancing out of my reach, reminding me how far I must go to bring comfort to my people."

"This may surprise you," said the captain, "but I thought of them that way, too, for a little while."

He turned to her. "You did?"

"Yes. You see, my crew and I are more than seventy thousand light-years from our home galaxy."

He looked at her, barely able to wrap his mind

around such a distance. "How did you come to stray so far?"

"It's a long story," she told him. "Suffice it to say we didn't come here of our own free will. And when we realized how long it would take us to get back, we were daunted—to say the least."

Rahmin grunted softly. "I'm not surprised."

"But in time," Janeway said, "we realized an opportunity had been set before us. We were in a part of the universe that had never been explored by our people. We had a chance to see phenomena, life-forms and civilizations that none of our people had ever seen before."

The Caatati smiled. "A chance to explore."

"That's right," she said. "And that's when the stars stopped looking like our enemies."

Rahmin glanced again at the points of light in the darkness. "Perhaps that will happen some day for the Caatati as well. It would be a pleasant change, I assure you."

"Captain?" came a voice over the intercom.

"Janeway here. What is it, B'Elanna?"

"A small problem," the engineer reported. "One of the impulse engines has developed a variance in its driver-coil assembly. I'm going to have to shut it down until I can make adjustments."

Janeway frowned. That was a two-man job, and only B'Elanna and Lt. Carey had the expertise to do it quickly.

"So there'll be a delay in the thorium project," the captain concluded.

"I'm afraid so. I'll put Vorik on it, but as you know, he's had no experience with isotope generation."

"Acknowledged," Janeway told her. "We'll sit tight."

Rahmin's face was a silent question. Obviously, he was concerned about the delay, perhaps even to the point of wondering if the isotopes would be generated at all.

"Don't worry," the captain told him. "We'll produce those isotopes for you. It's just a matter of time."

The Caatati seemed to accept that. But then, Janeway remarked inwardly, it wasn't as if he was likely to find a *better* offer.

B'Elanna headed back to engineering with a certain amount of impatience. Her companion seemed to notice it.

"Eager to get back?" Carey asked.

"Damned right," she told him.

After all, B'Elanna had promised the captain that thorium for the Caatati. Having to deal with the variance in the driver coil had been an annoyance she could have lived without.

Fortunately, the driver-coil problem had turned out to be less complicated than B'Elanna expected. She and Carey had finished the job in a little under an hour.

Now, she thought, she could devote her full attention to the thorium project—unless something else went wrong. And considering what day it was, she wasn't ruling anything out.

A moment later, B'Elanna walked into engineering. As she looked around, she noticed Seven of Nine standing off to the side. Though she might have been standing there for a while, the Borg looked unperturbed.

Something stiffened in the lieutenant. After all, this was *her* place, and had been for the last few years. She didn't appreciate intruders in engineering—especially the kind that had murdered and assimilated their way through the galaxy.

Since Chakotay had pulled rank on her, B'Elanna had no choice but to let Seven of Nine work there. But she didn't have to like it.

If the Borg had any idea of how her superior felt about her, she didn't show it. Approaching the lieutenant, she said, "I am reporting for duty." Her face was a mask of equanimity.

How lovely for you, B'Elanna thought. But what she said was, "Commander Chakotay told me to expect you."

"Where may I work?" asked Seven of Nine.

Somewhere out of my sight, B'Elanna mused. But she didn't say *that* out loud either. Besides, engineering wasn't big enough for the Borg to conceal herself very well.

B'Elanna jerked a thumb at one of the consoles on the other side of the room—as far from her own console as possible. "That'll be your workstation," she told Seven of Nine. "You can conduct your computations there to your heart's content."

The Borg hesitated a moment, obviously unfamiliar with the expression. Still, she must have gotten the gist of it, because she didn't ask any more questions. She simply made her way to the workstation.

As B'Elanna watched, Seven of Nine inspected the console. Then she tapped out a few commands on its keypadd. Her eyes moved in tandem with the data scrolling across the screen.

At least she's obedient, B'Elanna mused. She may be sabotaging the ship, but she's doing it politely.

Suddenly, the Borg looked up and saw the engineer staring at her. "This will be satisfactory," she said.

"Good," said B'Elanna. "If you're happy, I'm happy."

Her sarcasm was apparently lost on Seven of Nine. The Borg had no reaction that the lieutenant could discern. She just turned back to her screen and began to make her calculations.

The engineer shook her head. Then, forgetting about the Borg for the moment, she approached Vorik. He was working at his usual console.

"How are those thorium isotopes coming?" she asked.

The Vulcan stopped to look at her. He didn't look happy. "I will admit I am having trouble, Lieutenant."

"What sort of trouble?"

"Controlling the neutron absorption," he said.

B'Elanna pondered the problem. "Try increasing the temperature of the plasma above the neutron-activation threshold. That ought to help."

Vorik's brow creased as he considered his superior's approach. "Yes. I can see how it would."

She smiled. "Let's get that thorium to the captain as soon as it's ready."

The Vulcan nodded. "I will do that."

Leaving him to his labors, B'Elanna moved to the next workstation and then the one after that, seeing if there were any other difficulties that had arisen in her absence. There weren't.

Finally, she approached Seven of Nine. After all, the Borg was engaged in a project of particular interest to the captain. If she was approaching some aspect of the problem the wrong way, B'Elanna couldn't just let her founder. She would have to set her on the right path again, just as she would do with anyone else in her section.

"How's it going?" she asked Seven of Nine, trying to keep the rancor out of her voice.

The Borg looked at her with that empty expression of hers. "I am doing well," she responded.

Her tone was matter-of-fact, almost devoid of inflection. There was something about it that grated badly on B'Elanna's nerves—something that made her want to wring some emotion out of Seven of Nine.

"I'm glad to hear it," the engineer replied. She sized the Borg up. "Tell me something, Seven of Nine."

"Of course."

B'Elanna knew she shouldn't be asking the question. She asked it anyway. "When you hear about people like the Caatati, a race that was all but destroyed by the Borg . . . do you have any feelings of remorse? Do you regret what you did to them?"

Seven of Nine's eyes seemed to lose their focus for a moment. She seemed to be searching for the appropriate response.

Finally, she came up with one. "No."

B'Elanna eyed her. She wasn't sure what kind of answer she had expected, but that wasn't it. "That's it? Just . . . 'no'?"

Seven of Nine regarded her with that cold, distant gaze of hers. "What further answer do you require?"

The engineer stared at the Borg. "Oh, maybe some kind of acknowledgment of the billions of lives you've helped to destroy . . . a justification for what you did." She shook her head. "Maybe a little sense of guilt . . ."

"Guilt is irrelevant," Seven of Nine told her.

B'Elanna frowned. "Heartwarming."

The Borg regarded her. "An animal in the wild doesn't feel remorse for slaughtering its kill."

B'Elanna could feel the vitriol rising within her. "That's about what I'd expect from an unfeeling machine."

Seven of Nine was neither hurt nor offended . . . nor anything else. Completely unmoved, she gestured to indicate her console. "I have set up the parameters for the tachyon burst we'll need to create a transwarp conduit."

The lieutenant grunted. The Borg was fast, she'd give her that.

Seven of Nine went on. "It will be several hours before the main deflector can be modified accordingly. I think it would be best if I waited in my alcove in the meantime."

B'Elanna nodded. That was the best idea she'd heard yet. "I think you're right," she told the Borg.

Seven of Nine turned and headed for the exit. The sliding doors parted and then closed behind her, leaving B'Elanna alone with her feelings.

The most immediate one was regret. After all, the captain had taken Seven of Nine under her wing. She had tried to make the Borg feel comfortable on

Voyager, tried to help her remember what it was like to be human.

Not that B'Elanna agreed with any of that. As far as she was concerned, a Borg was a Borg was a Borg. But it wasn't her place to try to goad Seven of Nine into a confrontation.

What the hell was I thinking? the lieutenant asked herself. *I'm not a brat with a chip on her shoulder any longer. I'm a professional. I should be able to control my emotions.*

Next time, she promised herself, she would do a damned sight better—even if she had to have herself gagged and bound to the warp core to do it.

As Neelix directed the packaging and deployment of the various foodstuffs he'd set aside for the Caatati, he saw Captain Janeway walk in with Rahmin at her side. The alien seemed amazed at the size of the cargo hold where all this was taking place.

Obviously, Janeway had discounted Tuvok's concerns about Rahmin coming aboard the ship. And rightly so, Neelix thought. He'd seen his share of strangers in his day, and none of them seemed half as much in need of help as the Caatati.

Turning to Ensign Parke, who was shoving half a bale of *m'binda* grass into a container, the Talaxian said, "I'll be right back."

Parke nodded patiently. "Take your time," she said, her blue eyes sparkling beneath brown hair. "I've got plenty to do until you get back."

Neelix took a look at the other bale of *m'binda* grass in the ensign's vicinity, as well as the piles of *maqnorra* leaves and *snorrla* bark. "Yes," he said, "I guess you do."

Then he made his way across the hold to join the captain and the Caatati. They seemed pleased to see him—especially Rahmin.

"Things seem to be going well," the alien noted.

"They are," Neelix agreed. "Of course, it's a lot of work, but fortunately, we've got a lot of willing hands to help with it."

"And as I've just told Rahmin," Janeway added, "we're generating lots of thorium for him in engineering."

"Ah, yes," said the Talaxian. He had an idea. "Say, wouldn't our guest be interested to see how Lieutenant Torres—"

The captain gave him a funny look.

"—is generating those isotopes?" he finished.

"Actually," Janeway replied, "it's a rather mundane procedure. Besides, Lieutenant Torres's time is better spent producing thorium than conducting tours of engineering."

Neelix wondered at the tone of her voice. "But—"

"No buts about it," the captain told him. "Especially when I think Rahmin would be a great deal *more* intrigued by our airponics bay."

Obviously, the Talaxian concluded, something was going on. He didn't know what it was, but it seemed best to play along with it.

"I imagine that's true," he answered. "The airponics bay is something you have to see to believe."

"And the Caatati can use all the growing techniques they can get their hands on," Janeway pointed out.

Rahmin nodded. "We certainly can."

"Then we'll make that our next stop," the captain decided. She turned to the Talaxian. "Keep up the good work, Mr. Neelix."

He shrugged. "I'll do my best."

A moment later, Janeway and the Caatati had departed. Neelix stood there, scratching his head. "I don't get it," he muttered.

"Don't get what?" asked Ensign Parke, who had come up beside him.

"Why the captain wouldn't want our friend Rahmin to see engineering," he replied. "After all, it's one of the most interesting parts of the ship. And it *is* where the isotopes are being produced."

Parke chuckled. "Are you serious?"

The Talaxian looked at her. "What do you mean?"

"The Borg were the ones who almost destroyed the Caatati—right?"

He nodded. "Right."

"And Seven of Nine is a Borg."

Neelix smacked his forehead with the heel of his hand. "Of course—Seven of Nine is working in engineering now. What kind of idiot am I not to have thought of that?"

Parke regarded him sympathetically. "As far as I can tell, a very well-meaning idiot." She pointed across the hold at the containers she'd been working on. "So, I've got the *m'binda* grass, the *maqnorra* leaves and the *snorrla* bark packed away. What's next?"

The Talaxian stroked his chin judiciously. "How about the *granik* roots?"

The ensign smiled again. "Your wish is my command."

And she left Neelix to think about the horrific faux pas he'd almost made. Imagine Rahmin bumping into Seven of Nine, he thought. What a disaster *that* would have been.

CHAPTER
7

THE CAPTAIN STOOD BETWEEN NEELIX AND TUVOK AND watched Rahmin take his place on the transporter grid. As the Caatati did so, he smiled at her.

Janeway had seldom seen anyone as happy or as grateful as Rahmin was at that moment. Of course, as he had told her again and again, the captain and crew of *Voyager* had given his people more than supplies. They had given the Caatati new hope—and it was hard to place a value on that.

"I cannot thank you enough," Rahmin said.

"You already have," Janeway assured him. "Many times over, I assure you. Good luck, my friend. I hope you find what you're looking for."

Neelix nodded. "Me, too."

Tuvok raised his hand in the splay-fingered Vulcan salute. "Live long and prosper," he told the Caatati.

Rahmin inclined his head. "With the help of people like you," he said, "I will endeavor to do just that."

The captain turned to the transporter operator, a blond woman named Burleson. "Energize." After all, Janeway added silently, there's only so much gratitude a person can take.

"Aye, Captain," said Burleson. Her fingers moved over her control board with practiced precision.

A moment later, a corruscating pattern of light enveloped Rahmin. Then both he and the light pattern vanished.

Janeway tapped her commbadge. "Commander Chakotay?"

"Chakotay here, Captain."

"I'm on my way back to the bridge. The Caatati should be going their own way any moment now."

"Acknowledged," said the first officer.

"So," Neelix remarked, "the Caatati were everything they claimed they were—refugees in need of assistance." He turned to Tuvok. "You see, Mr. Vulcan? Your fears were unfounded."

Tuvok's brow furrowed ever so slightly. "As security officer, I'm required to take precautions against all potential threats," he explained. "Despite their apparent neediness, the Caatati were unknown to us. Thus, they, too, had the potential to become a threat."

"But they didn't," the Talaxian pointed out.

"But they *could* have," the Vulcan countered.

"Gentlemen," said Janeway, "the Caatati are water under the bridge. If you don't mind, I'd like to move on."

Tuvok thrust his chin out. "Of course."

"Fine with me," Neelix replied cheerfully.

Chuckling to herself, Janeway led the way out of the transporter room. Tuvok and Neelix were such opposites. She wondered if any other captain had ever had to put up with a bickering pair like that.

Agron Lumas sat on the edge of his bed, in the cramped, Spartan quarters that were the best his ship had to offer, and considered the realizor he had salvaged from the wreck of his world.

The device no longer looked new. Its band had been bent, its sleek, dark metal tarnished in places. But it still worked.

The question was . . . did he want to use it? Sometimes Lumas regretted that he'd taken it with him. All it ever brought him was pain and guilt, after all. But if pain and guilt were all he had . . .

With trembling fingers, he lifted the thing to the level of his head. Then he put it on and closed his eyes.

Lumas thought of a picnic on the shore of the Aranatoc Sea. His wife was there—not as he had seen her last, but with a smile on her face. Finaea was there as well, just a few days shy of her tenth birthday. And sweet little Anyelot was only six, her thin shoulders browned by the sun.

He felt a lump in his throat, but he swallowed it away. After all, his wife and daughters would be concerned if they saw sadness in his eyes, and Lumas desperately didn't want to ruin their picnic.

Opening his eyes, he saw his memories had come to life, there in the confines of his cabin. His loved ones were as warm and tangible as he was—and a good deal healthier looking. If nothing else, they had been spared the miseries their world's survivors had been forced to endure.

At least, Lumas thought, there was *that* very small consolation.

"Father?" said Finaea, her face full of innocence.

He smiled at her. "Yes, child?"

"You've barely touched your *ranghia.*"

Lumas looked down at the bowl that had appeared in his hands. It was full of an aromatic orange puree—one that made his stomach growl as loudly as if the food were real.

"No," he said, "I haven't, have I?" He held the bowl out to his daughter, just as he had done that day at the shore. "Would you like some of it?"

Finaea's face lit up—then dimmed again. "I don't want to take it if you want it, Father."

But Lumas knew that she *did* want it. Even at that age, she was too considerate to say so.

"It's all right," he told her. "I'm not very hungry right now."

At the time, he hadn't been lying. He had eaten too much the night before. Now, it took a great deal of willpower to hand Finaea the bowl of *ranghia,* even if it *wasn't* real.

But hand it over he did. It was the least he could do for his daughter, now that she had become . . . whatever it was she had become. Again, he felt the lump in his throat, and this time it was much harder to make it go away.

"Agron," said his wife, "are you all right?"

It was one of the most wondrous things about the

realizor—that it could ascertain the mood of the user and make it manifest to his or her creations. Lumas shook his head and held his hand out to his wife.

"I'm fine," he said. "It's just the seamotes. You know how they tickle my nose this time of year."

Looking at his wife, Lumas wanted to say more. He wanted to tell her how much he missed her. He wanted to say how badly he felt that he hadn't done more to keep her safe.

Instead, he added, "Where's that libation we packed? I'm in the mood for a good celebration. In fact—"

Suddenly, Lumas realized the door was open. Sedrek, his second-in-command, was standing at the threshold.

"Excuse me," he said, "but we're in communications range."

Immediately, Lumas wrenched the realizor from his head, making his family blink out of existence. For a moment, he stared at the places his wife and children had occupied, feeling once again the terrible, heartwrenching pain of losing them.

Then he gathered himself and turned back to Sedrek. The man made no mention of the realizor-generated apparitions.

"Let's go," said Lumas.

He got up, his limbs heavy but far from useless. Fortunately, the realizor's debilitating afteraffects diminished with frequent use. And in the time since the Borg attack, he imagined he must have employed the device a hundred times.

Still, Lumas was glad the bridge was just down the

corridor. Making his way to the bridge with Sedrek a step behind him, he entered the room and turned expectantly to the viewscreen.

Rahmin looked back at Lumas. "Ah," he said. "There you are."

There was no love lost between Lumas and Rahmin. Though their paths had crossed several times since they left the Caatati homeworld, they seldom agreed on a course long enough to remain in contact.

To Lumas's way of thinking, survival was survival. One did whatever it took to go on and enable his followers to do the same. One didn't stand on principle when lives hung in the balance.

Rahmin, on the other hand, believed in dealing fairly and openly. To him, it was more important to be honest than to endure.

But then, Rahmin had been a teacher on their world. A gentle, unassuming soul with no appetite for conflict.

Once, as a young man, Rahmin had served as technician on a far-reaching Caatati spaceflight. It was that fact that evidently had earned him command of his survivor vessel.

But since his youth, Rahmin had merely helped *train* technicians. His practical knowledge was actually quite limited—and his leadership abilities, in Lumas's view, were virtually nonexistent.

Lumas, by contrast, had been a man of accomplishment, a builder. He was better suited to solving complex and difficult problems—sometimes in ways the squeamish did not approve of.

"So," he said, eyeing the image of Rahmin on the screen. "We meet again, my friend. And, as I understand it, none too soon."

The other man's eyes narrowed. "What do you mean?"

Lumas shrugged. "I've heard you had dealings with a ship called *Voyager*. And that you profited by the experience."

"Who told you that?" asked Rahmin.

"Traders," said Lumas. "They had offered to take one of our ships off our hands, in exchange for a quantity of food. When I declined their offer and suggested something more equitable, they remarked that the Caatati were not nearly as desperate as they had heard. Why, a ship commanded by someone named Rahmin had actually spurned them altogether."

He tapped his chin with a forefinger, pretending to give the matter some thought. "Now, how could a Caatati vessel reject a trader out of hand? Especially when that trader might have food and medicine, which it would be willing to exchange for spare engine parts?"

Lumas acted as if he had suddenly been struck with an idea. "Unless, of course, that same Caatati vessel had all the food and medicine it needed. And perhaps a supply of thorium isotopes as well."

Rahmin's eyes grew wide with trepidation. "You'll not get our thorium," he declared. "Even if there *are* three of you to our one."

Lumas shook his head. "Generosity was never one of your best qualities, my friend. But don't worry.

You need not part with your newfound wealth. All you have to do is tell me where to find this treasure-laden *Voyager*."

Rahmin hesitated. "They treated us well. Too well to send the likes of *you* after them, Lumas."

Lumas flushed with indignation. "The likes of *me?*" he raged. "Have you forgotten where you come from, Rahmin? Or that I came from the same place? Does the same blood not run in *both* our veins?" He gestured to his bridge technicians. "And theirs as well?"

The Caatati on the viewscreen looked pained by the accusation—just as Lumas had intended. Now was the time to press his case.

"We're all Caatati," Lumas said in a softer voice. "All victims of the same devastation. If we can't help each other, Rahmin, do we still deserve to survive at all?"

Rahmin swallowed. "Perhaps you're right," he replied contritely. He looked down. "Forgive me, Lumas. We've been wandering so long, living hand to mouth, I've forgotten what common decency is."

Lumas smiled. "Then you'll help us?"

The other Caatati nodded. "Yes. Of course. As you so aptly put it, the same blood runs through all of us. May you have as much luck with Captain Janeway as I did."

Turning to one of his own technicians, Rahmin said, "Transmit the coordinates where we encountered *Voyager*. And also her heading at the point when we left her." He turned back to Lumas. "That's the best we can do."

Lumas inclined his head. "Then it will have to be enough."

And it *would* be, he thought. He and his fellow survivors would find this *Voyager*. And when they did, they would be as well off as Rahmin's bunch.

Maybe better.

CHAPTER
8

B'ELANNA SAT IN A FUNK AT A TABLE IN *VOYAGER*'S MESS hall, picking at her lunch in a desultory fashion. Nothing was going her way.

And the day was still young. Who knew what horrors awaited her before it was over?

Out of the corner of her eye, she saw Neelix coming her way. The engineer sighed. The Talaxian was no doubt bent on cheering her up. Little did he know what he was up against.

"My, my," said Neelix. "If ever I saw a job for the morale officer, it's sitting right here."

Some time ago, the captain had given him that honorary position on the ship. The Talaxian took it seriously, too—almost always to good effect. But not this time, B'Elanna thought.

She tried to smile, but it didn't come out right. "I

don't think you've ever faced a greater challenge, Neelix."

"I *enjoy* a challenge," the Talaxian told her.

Then Neelix brought something out from behind his back—something he had been holding there without her realizing it. It was a small bowl full of something noxious-looking. B'Elanna wrinkled her nose.

"Is that supposed to make me feel better?" she asked.

"Blood pie," the Talaxian said—as if any explanation was necessary. "In honor of the Day of Honor."

Neelix was acting as if this were the first time they had ever discussed the Klingon holiday. It wasn't, of course.

The year before, he had tried to commemorate the Day of Honor by serving her a surprise assortment of Klingon dishes—*rokeg* blood pie, serpent worms, heart of *targ,* and the like. And she had stalked out of the mess hall, not caring to be reminded of the holiday.

So why was Neelix standing there with a smile on his face, proudly holding out the bowl of *rokeg* blood pie?

She narrowed her eyes. "Has Tom been talking to you?"

"Not at all," said Neelix. "I am nothing if not persistent."

"Are you really?" the engineer asked.

"Yes," he said, setting down the bowl. "And if I'm correct, many Klingon families traditionally serve *rokeg* blood pie on the Day of Honor."

"How interesting," she replied, smiling. "I appreciate the gesture, Neelix—but I've decided to ignore the Day of Honor."

The Talaxian was surprised. "Oh? But what about the ritual you prepared in the holodeck?"

B'Elanna stared at him, amazed. "You know about that?"

He shrugged.

She shook her head. "I'm going to kill Tom when I see him."

"Actually," said Neelix, "it was Ensign Kim who told me."

The lieutenant made a sound deep in her throat. "Look," she said, "I thought I had shaken the bad luck that used to dog me every year on the Day of Honor. Now, I see I was mistaken. My bad luck is back—with a vengeance.

"So no *rokeg* blood pie," B'Elanna said. "No examining my behavior over the last year to see if I measure up to Klingon standards of honor. Let's just forget the Day of Honor ever existed, all right?"

She was serious. She hoped her look told him so.

Neelix swept the bowl of *rokeg* blood pie off the table. "Understood," he responded cheerfully.

The Talaxian started away from the table, then stopped himself. He turned back to her. "Lieutenant," he said, "without prying into the cause of the, er, black cloud that's hanging over you, may I suggest something—based on my observations of you over the months we've served on *Voyager* together?"

"Go right ahead," B'Elanna told him.

Neelix pulled out a chair and sat down with her. "It seems to me," he said, "you have a bit of a temper . . . that you try to keep reined in, but sometimes all those feelings build up in you until you explode at someone."

She frowned. "I'd say that about sums it up."

"Well," the Talaxian went on, "I'm offering to be a pressure valve."

B'Elanna tilted her head. "A what?"

"A pressure valve," he repeated. "You may use me to blow off steam. When you're angry or feeling stressed, come see me. Call me names. Insult me."

"Neelix," she said. "I—"

"Even question my parentage," he told her. "Give me a tongue-lashing like you've never given anyone before. I promise I won't take it personally. And," he said, leaning closer to her, "you won't have to keep things bottled up inside anymore."

The engineer regarded him fondly. Then she reached out and covered his hand with hers.

"That's probably the nicest offer I've gotten in a long time. Thank you, Neelix. You're awfully sweet. But I'm not sure I could do that to you."

He looked back at her with what was obviously genuine affection. "Well," he said, "I'm here if you need me. Remember that."

Rising from his chair, he started off. B'Elanna watched him go, touched by his concern for her.

"Neelix?" she said.

He stopped and turned back to her. "Yes?"

"About this Day of Honor program," the engineer said. "Do you think I should go through with it?"

The Talaxian returned to her table. "I've always thought traditions were good things. That is, worth preserving."

B'Elanna sighed. "I've been thinking a lot about the

rituals my mother taught me, and they don't seem so hateful as they did when I was a child. Maybe being so far away from anything Klingon has changed me."

"It certainly can't hurt to go through with the ceremony," he told her.

She looked at him. "I don't know what effect it'll have on me. That's what's so frightening."

Neelix gave her a smile of encouragement and put his hand over hers. He didn't say anything more—but then, he didn't have to.

"All right," said B'Elanna. "Bring on the *rokeg* blood pie. I can do this."

The Talaxian winked at her. Returning the bowl, he stood there and watched her dig in.

The Caves of Kahless were filled with thousands of long, twisted candles and a collection of guttering torches. As B'Elanna negotiated a path among them, a tendril of fog wrapped around her like a giant snake.

She breathed in the cool, dank air. It carried a metallic scent. Like a *bat'leth*. Or blood.

It hardly mattered to the engineer that this was a holodeck program. It seemed real. And the farther she delved into the earth, the more real it became for her.

Tom did a good job on this, she thought. He must really have put his heart and soul into it. It made her even more certain that she had done the right thing by trying out the program.

B'Elanna wound her way from one cave to the other. Each one contained the same torches, the same candles, the same sinuous drifts of fog. But to Tom's credit, no two caves were exactly alike.

Finally, she reached the cavern she was seeking.

Three tall, muscular Klingons awaited her inside, their bare shoulders festooned with braids of their smoky, dark hair. B'Elanna approached them tentatively, not really knowing much about the ritual that would follow.

After all, she had only had a small part in the program's design. Tom had done the rest, drawing on authentic Klingon traditions.

"Qapla'! I am Moklor the Interrogator," said the tallest of the Klingons, his very tone an invitation to combat. "What warrior goes there?"

"My name's B'Elanna," she answered.

Moklor's grey eyes narrowed beneath his brow ridge. "Have you come to have your honor challenged?"

She shrugged. "I guess so, yes."

"Are you willing to see the ceremony through to the end?"

"That's the idea, isn't it? What do I do?" B'Elanna asked.

"It will be a lengthy ordeal," the interrogator told her. "First, you must eat from the heart of a sanctified *targ.*"

He gestured and one of the other Klingons brought forth a platter. There were several lumps of raw, lavender-colored meat on it. The Klingon presented the platter to B'Elanna.

"Pak lohr!" bellowed Moklor.

The engineer had never been a fan of Klingon food, and *rokeg* blood pie was tame compared to heart of *targ.* Steeling herself, she picked up one of the lumps of meat and put it in her mouth. Then, with an effort, she chewed.

The interrogator nodded approvingly. "The heart of a *targ* brings courage to the one who eats it. Next," he said, "you will drink *mot'loch* from the grail of Kahless."

He gestured, and the warrior who held the platter of *targ* meat backed away into shadow. At the same time, another Klingon stepped forward into the light. He was carrying a large metal cup.

As he handed it to B'Elanna, she sniffed it. It didn't smell pleasant by anyone's standards.

Moklor's eyes opened wide. "Drink to the glory of Kahless, the greatest warrior of all time."

B'Elanna took the cup and swallowed back her nausea. Then she forced herself to drink the noxious concoction.

The interrogator grinned as she handed the grail back to his helper. Obviously, the engineer thought, he was getting quite a kick out of this. It was nice to see someone enjoy his job so much.

"Kahless defeated his enemies on the field of battle," Moklor intoned, "and built a mighty empire." He regarded B'Elanna. "How have *you* proven yourself worthy of the name Klingon?"

She considered the question. Not being particularly devoted to her Klingon heritage, she had never asked herself anything like it before.

"Well," B'Elanna said at last, "I haven't built any empires lately—or at all, in fact. But not so long ago, I forced an entire culture to admit it had committed genocide."

Moklor looked puzzled. "In what way was that a Klingon deed?"

"I didn't let them sweep millions of deaths under a rug," she explained. "I made them acknowledge what they had done."

Moklor still didn't seem to get it. "But . . . what battles have you fought? How many enemies have you defeated?"

"I can't say I've *personally* defeated any," B'Elanna responded—a little lamely, she thought. "But the crew of my ship was able to dispel an army of warriors from another dimension."

Moklor scowled. Obviously, he was still unimpressed.

"You have to realize," the engineer went on, "I'm not living among warriors. That limits my opportunities a bit."

The interrogator spat. "Then how do you expect to distinguish yourself as a Klingon warrior?"

A good question, she thought. At least, from Moklor's point of view. "I don't really know. I guess I'm doing the best I can."

"What of your enemies?" the interrogator asked. "Have they been more worthy of a warrior's attention?"

B'Elanna frowned. "Worthy?"

"Strong," Moklor elaborated. "And honorable."

She chuckled grimly. "Frankly, I haven't seen a whole lot of honor in my enemies. Take the Borg, for instance—a race of unfeeling, machinelike monsters. They assimilate one species after another, destroy whole worlds full of innocents. Oh, they're strong, all right. They're absolutely deadly. But from where I stand, I'd say they don't rack up many honor points."

Moklor pondered her answer, his eyes gleaming in the firelight. "Those acts alone are not dishonorable," he concluded.

Frustrated, B'Elanna shook her head. She had never comprehended Klingon ways, and apparently she never would.

"Well, then," she said, "maybe I don't understand the notion of honor. Maybe I don't *want* to understand it. Maybe this is all . . . I don't know . . . just meaningless gibberish."

Moklor shook his head reproachfully. "A pitiful reply."

The engineer did her best to control her annoyance. "You think so?"

The interrogator nodded slowly. "Let us proceed."

B'Elanna didn't say anything. She just waited for whatever came next.

Moklor lifted his bearded chin. "A warrior must endure great hardship. To test your mettle, you will undergo the Ritual of Twenty Painstiks. After that, you will engage in combat a master of the *bat'leth*. Finally, you will traverse the sulfurous lagoons of Gorath . . ."

B'Elanna held a hand up. "You know," she said, "I don't think so. I mean, I didn't want to do any of this stuff *before* you described it. I certainly don't want to do it now."

She inclined her head. "Have a good day, Interrogator. I'm leaving."

B'Elanna started to go around him, but Moklor barred her way. His eyes bulged and turned red with fury as he answered her.

"Not until you have completed the ceremony, *p'tahk.*"

Then he grabbed her shoulders, to make good on his threat. Surprised, B'Elanna cursed and tried to break Moklor's grip on her. But before she could get very far, two of his lackeys came out of the shadows with painstiks.

The devices were aptly named. The charge they sent through her made her feel as though she were being seared from within.

Howling with agony, B'Elanna shoved Moklor as hard as she could. He staggered backward, releasing her. Then she dropped into a crouch, ready to fight the other Klingons in the cave.

One of them assumed a *Mok'bara* stance, showing himself to be a practitioner of the Klingon martial art. He approached B'Elanna with his hands held out in front of him, moving in a rhythmic pattern.

Before she knew it, he had gotten hold of her and flipped her on her back. The impact against the hard stone took her breath away for a moment. Looking up, B'Elanna saw her adversary aiming a blow at her face.

She rolled just in time to avoid it. The Klingon hit the cavern floor instead of her, causing him to cry out in pain. As he grasped his injured hand, B'Elanna scrambled to her feet and straightened him up with a two-fisted punch. A second punch laid the warrior out cold.

Her lips drawn back, B'Elanna confronted Moklor's other helper. He seemed less eager to tackle her than the first one.

The engineer glared at Moklor. "Thanks so much," she told him. "It's been lovely. But we won't be doing it again some time."

The interrogator's mouth twisted with anger. He pointed a long, gnarled finger at her. "You cannot leave! You have yet to complete the ceremony!"

But B'Elanna stalked out of the place. She'd had dumb ideas before, she told herself, but this was by far the dumbest.

CHAPTER

9

B'ELANNA WAS LYING IN A FETAL POSITION ON THE COUCH in her quarters when she heard the door chime. Go away, she thought.

But what she said was, "Come in."

The door slid aside, revealing her visitor. It was Tom.

He looked at her lying there. "Are you all right?" he asked.

With an effort, B'Elanna sat up. "I'm fine."

"I tried to find you before," Tom explained. "But you were in the holodeck."

"That's right."

Tom frowned. "I gathered as much. You know you left it running? There was a Klingon in there who didn't look too happy."

B'Elanna grunted. "Really."

"Yeah," said Tom. "He was nursing a whale of a black eye. Looks like he had a run-in with someone who's having a bad day."

She frowned at him. "Very funny."

Tom didn't say anything more for a while. It seemed to B'Elanna that he was waiting for her to talk about the program. Of course, that was the *last* thing she wanted to talk about.

"So," he said finally, "how did it go?"

"It didn't," the engineer replied, unable to keep the pique out of her voice. "Do you mind if we talk about something else?"

Tom regarded her—first with surprise, then with a certain resolve. "As a matter of fact," he told her, "I do. You've been spitting like a cobra all day. And frankly, it's getting boring."

"Is it?" B'Elanna muttered, looking away.

"It sure as hell *is*. We designed that holodeck program together, if you recall, and I think you owe me the courtesy of telling me what happened."

She looked up at him. "It was ridiculous—a lot of meaningless posturing. Honor, dishonor . . . what does it matter, anyway?"

Tom's eyes narrowed. "It matters because it's part of who you are. You've been running away from that all your life."

Anger flared in her, sudden and white-hot. "Who are *you* to tell me that?" B'Elanna wondered.

"I care about you," the flight controller told her bluntly. "I care what happens to you. But if you keep pushing me away, there's not much point in my sticking around—is there?"

She shrugged. "Fine. Leave me alone, then." Purely out of spite, she gestured toward the door.

Tom darkened with rage. "Don't worry," he said. "If this is the way you treat people who try to be your friend, you'll be alone, all right. You'll be *all* alone."

Then, with a hard look, he turned and left her quarters. The door whispered closed in his wake.

Suddenly, B'Elanna realized what a child she had been. She let her head sink into her hands.

Good going, she thought. There's only one living being on the ship who has an outside chance of understanding what you're going through—and you just sent him away.

Maybe Moklor had been right. Maybe she *was* a *p'tahk.*

Lt. Carey put his tools away and massaged his shoulder where a muscle had tightened up on him. Then he replaced the bulkhead plate that covered the replicator circuitry.

For the last time, he thought. At least, I *hope* it's for the last time.

Tapping his commbadge, he said, "Carey to Lt. Torres."

"Torres here," came the response.

"Listen," he said, "Lt. Paris mentioned that his replicator wasn't working. I could've waited until it turned up on the assignment list—"

"But you didn't," said Torres. "You just fixed it. Even though you're supposed to be off-duty."

"Basically, yes. I figured that's what you would have done."

"You figured right," she assured him. "Good work, Carey. Just don't rest on your laurels."

"I never do," he reminded her.

And that was that. Carey smiled and shook his head.

Before *Voyager* left Earth orbit a few years earlier, he was second-in-command in the engineering section. Then the ship got shunted into the Delta Quadrant, and his chief was killed in the process.

For a while, Carey figured he was the only one capable of being in charge of engineering. Then Torres moved in, with her take-no-prisoners approach. Naturally, they banged heads.

He was just standing up for what he thought was best—not only for himself, but for everyone on the ship. Unfortunately for him, Torres wasn't buying any of it. Finally, she brought the matter to a boil.

She broke his nose in three places.

Naturally, Carey thought the captain would stand by him. After all, his Starfleet record was impeccable. But Janeway had her own problems to contend with. *Voyager* was no longer purely a Starfleet ship—not with a contingent of Maquis aboard.

When he heard the captain was even considering Torres for the engineering post, he nearly ruptured a blood vessel—and not in his nose. After all, she was an ex-Maquis—someone who had attended the Academy for a while but couldn't cut it. Or so he had heard.

In the end, the captain didn't give in to pressure from anyone. She picked the best person for the job— and that person was B'Elanna Torres. Eventually, even Carey agreed with the choice.

Since that time, Torres had distinguished herself over and over again. And Carey, as her first assistant, had served her as loyally as he had ever served any Starfleet lifer.

He had also gotten to know her as a friend as well as a colleague—and he knew when one of his friends was having a monster of a bad day. That's why he didn't mind fixing the replicator, even if he was supposed to be resting his weary bones.

"Day of Honor," he said out loud. "More like Day of Horror."

Only Klingons would put each other through such torture, he thought, as he picked up his tool case and headed for his quarters.

When the Doctor had the ship's computer place him in the holodeck, he believed he was visiting the Talaxian resort environment that had become so popular over the last few months—not only with himself, but with a majority of the crew.

As it turned out, he was wrong.

He found himself in a cave full of torches and twisted, tapering candles that struggled against wisps of fog. The Doctor looked around and saw that the cave connected with other caves, both in front and behind him. The other caves were full of candles and fog as well.

The Doctor harrumphed. "Either someone's been tinkering with the resort program," he observed sardonically, "or the holodeck is malfunctioning again." No doubt it was the latter.

Still, he mused, this milieu intrigued him. The Doctor wondered who had devised it and why. Unfortunately, there was no one present to provide answers to his questions. There were only the guttering candles, and they made no sound at all.

Then the Doctor heard what sounded like voices. Deep, gruff voices, speaking in some kind of rhythm. No doubt, the owners of those voices could shed some light on the situation.

"Well," he declared, "I'm not much of a spelunker. However, my curiosity has been aroused."

With that, he made his way in the direction of the voices. As it turned out, their source was closer than he had imagined. By the time he had traversed his third cavern, he caught sight of three tall, swarthy figures. They glared at him from beneath bony brow ridges.

"Klingons," the Doctor concluded. "How charming."

His direct experience with the species had been limited to his interactions with Lieutenant Torres. Those interactions had been positive ones, for the most part.

However, the Doctor's program included a great many references to Klingon culture and psychology. It didn't require any mental gymnastics for him to realize he might have placed himself in a sticky situation.

Of course, this was only a holodeck program. He could stop it any time he liked. With that assurance in mind, he approached the Klingons and inclined his head.

"Greetings," said the Doctor. He flashed a smile. "If I may ask, what exactly is your function here?"

The largest of them stepped forward. *"Qapla'!* I

am Moklor the Interrogator. What warrior goes there?"

"I'm not a warrior," the Doctor answered. "I'm a physician."

Moklor looked at him askance. "What is your name?" he insisted.

The Doctor sighed. "I haven't selected a name yet. In the meantime, you may refer to me as the Emergency Medical Hologram."

The Klingon didn't seem pleased with that option. He cast glances left and right at his underlings.

"Or," the hologram suggested, "you may call me the Doctor."

Moklor didn't seem thrilled with that option either. However, he appeared to accept it. "Have you come to have your honor challenged?" he asked, his eyes narrowing.

"My . . . honor?" the Doctor repeated.

"Your honor!" the interrogator thundered. The word echoed throughout the cave as if it had been shouted by a chorus.

"Er . . . yes," said the Doctor, seeing no harm in agreement. "Of course I have. Why not?"

"Are you willing to see the ceremony through to the end?" Moklor asked.

"That all depends."

"On what does it depend?" the interrogator asked him.

"On how long it takes. I've alotted myself an hour for recreation—no more than that. Anything beyond an hour and I'll have to take a rain check."

Moklor's brow furrowed. "A rayn'chek?"

"In other words," the Doctor explained, "I'll have

to continue the ceremony another time. Now, then . . . what's involved, exactly?"

Moklor's lip curled. "It will be a lengthy ordeal. First, you must eat from the heart of a sanctified *targ.*"

He gestured and one of his lackeys placed a platter in front of the Doctor. It held several lumps of bloody meat. As far as the Doctor was concerned, the sanctified *targ* could have had them back—with his compliments.

Still, he was inclined to be polite. "Mmm," he said. "They look delectable. My compliments to the chef."

"Pak lohr!" roared the interrogator.

"Er . . . whatever you say," the Doctor replied.

Picking up one of the bloody lumps, he ingested it. Actually, it wasn't as bad as it looked.

Moklor nodded as his underling withdrew with the platter. "The heart of a *targ* brings courage to the one who eats it. Next, you will drink *mot'loch* from the grail of Kahless."

A moment later, the interrogator's other helper came forward and produced a large metal cup. The Doctor took it from him and peered at the goopy brown liquid within it.

The Doctor had heard of a number of favorite Klingon beverages. *Mot'loch* was not one of them— and now he knew why. The smell of it alone was enough to make one retch.

Moklor raised his fist for emphasis. "Drink to the glory of Kahless, the greatest warrior of all time."

The Doctor sighed. He wasn't looking forward to this. However, he was rather curious as to how it all would turn out.

Steeling himself, he drank. Then he returned the cup to the interrogator, who passed it on to his lackey and grinned.

"Kahless defeated his enemies on the field of battle and built a mighty empire," he cried. Moklor eyed the Doctor. "How have *you* proven yourself worthy of the name Klingon?"

"Actually," the Doctor answered, "I'm not sure I *am* worthy—that is, of that particular name. Of course, I am no doubt worthy of a host of *other* titles and honorifics."

"It is only your worthiness as a Klingon that concerns me." As if to reinforce his point, the interrogator pounded his chest with his fist.

"Have it your way," said the Doctor. "But I'm still not sure how to respond to your inquiry."

Moklor considered him. "In what ways have you demonstrated your devotion to honor this last year?"

The Doctor chuckled. "My devotion to honor? Surely, you jest. It may interest you to know that I am an amalgam of the finest medical minds and personalities the Federation has ever known. It is absolutely impossible for me to do anything that is *less* than honorable."

Moklor looked unsatisfied. "But what have you *done?*"

The Doctor frowned. "I see. You require a list." He looked at the cavern's ceiling and gathered his thoughts. "All right. One year ago to the day, I stabilized and attended an Emmonite with severe burns over most of her body. Several days later, I treated Lieutenant Torres, Ensign Kim, and several other individuals, all of whom were suffering from radiation sickness. Later on that same week, I discovered a virus which—"

"No!" bellowed Moklor, his eyes blazing red with anger. "Speak of the battles you fought! Tell me the names of those you defeated!"

The Doctor harrumphed. "I believe I mentioned that I'm a physician. It's my job to preserve life, not to destroy it."

"You mock me?" said the Klingon, his hands turning into fists.

"Not at all," the Doctor told him warily.

Moklor regarded him with suspicion. "What of your enemies?" he asked. "Have they been worthy of a warrior's attention?"

The Doctor frowned. "No offense, but I don't think you've been listening very closely. I'm a physician. I heal people when they're sick. I have no enemies . . . unless, of course, you're speaking of the diseases I fight. But even then, it would be less than accurate to say—"

"You fight diseases?" the interrogator asked.

The Doctor paused. "That's one of my functions, yes."

"Deadly diseases?"

Once again, the Doctor could answer only one way. "Yes. Deadly ones."

"And you destroy them?"

The Doctor saw where Moklor was going with this. "As a matter of fact, I do. But I don't use a weapon."

The interrogator shrugged. "Weapons come in many forms. The important thing is that you confront your enemies and kill them. Now, how many of these diseases have you destroyed?"

The Doctor considered the question. "I don't know. Dozens? Hundreds?"

"Hundreds?" Moklor echoed. "And all by your hand?" He grinned. "Now *that* is a tale of honor worth the telling."

The Doctor had always thought so. And here, apparently, was someone willing to listen to it. In fact, it seemed to be the interrogator's job to listen to such accounts.

The Doctor was tempted to describe his victories over all manner of malady and bodily injury in protracted detail. However, it occurred to him that he still didn't know what this program was about.

"If you don't mind my asking," he told Moklor, "just what are we doing here? What's the function of an interrogator?"

The Klingon snorted. "An interrogator determines a warrior's worthiness on the Day of Honor."

"Ah," said the Doctor. *Now* he understood.

He had heard about the Day of Honor. It was a Klingon holiday established a century earlier, when a Starfleet captain by the name of Kirk helped rescue a planet full of Klingons.

Until then, Klingons had recognized honor only in one another. From that point on, they made it their business to celebrate honor in other species as well— even if those species were their enemies.

It brought up an interesting question. Since the first time the Doctor materialized on *Voyager,* he had been experimenting with the various traits and trappings of humanity, trying to find a combination that would define and even enhance his personality.

However, he had overlooked the value of embracing a holiday—or perhaps several of them. And yet, holidays seemed to have a valued place in the lives of the crew. Perhaps they might enrich his existence as well.

The more the Doctor thought about it, the more inclined he was to adopt a ritual celebration. The question was . . . which one?

The Day of Honor? He didn't think so. As interesting as his dialogue with Moklor had been, he didn't feel particularly moved by it. Then again, that was understandable. Klingon virtues were an acquired taste.

Some other holiday, then. The Bajoran Gratitude Festival, for instance. Or Cinco de Mayo, which Ensign Andujar had described in great detail. Or perhaps the Bolian Feast of Nineteen Sublime Pleasures.

There were so many. Clearly, in order to make an intelligent choice, he would have to embark on a rigorous schedule of experimentation. Only then could he find the celebration best suited to him.

Luckily, the Doctor boasted the expertise of the Federation's greatest scientists. No one could be better equipped to assess each holiday on its respective merits.

"Let us proceed," said Moklor. His gaze hardened. "A warrior must endure great hardship. To test your mettle, you will undergo the Ritual of Twenty Painstiks. After that, you will engage in combat with a master of the *bat'leth*. Finally, you will traverse the sulphurous lagoons of Gorath . . ."

"Perhaps some other time," the Doctor told him. He looked up at the stalactite-studded ceiling of the cavern. "Computer, terminate this program and return me to sickbay."

Abruptly, the Doctor found himself outside his office. Negotiating a path to his desk, he sat down at his terminal and brought up the information he needed. After a while, he smiled to himself.

"Now *that*," he said, "sounds intriguing."

CHAPTER

10

IT WASN'T SUSAN NICOLETTI'S IDEA TO SPEND HER DAY IN sickbay. But when she woke up shivering and saw the green blotches under her jawline, she hadn't had much choice but to see the Doctor.

Then she saw that Lt. Chafin had come down with the same virus. Something new to Federation science—and the biofilter as well, apparently.

The Doctor didn't have a name for it. He referred to it by a medical designation—delta nine-nine. His guess was that Nicoletti and Chafin had picked it up a week or so earlier, on one of the seedier space stations *Voyager* had run into.

A less versatile physician might have been thrown by the virus. Fortunately, the Doctor was as versatile as they came. In a matter of minutes, he had identified it, classified it, and come up with something to kill it.

The only problem was that the treatment was going to take four or five hours. But as the Doctor reminded Nicoletti and Chafin more than once, they were lucky to have a cure at all.

With no other option except to remain on her biobed, Nicoletti had eventually dozed off. When she woke up, the Doctor was standing beside her, a bemused expression on his face. Chafin, she noticed, was already gone.

"Is everything all right?" she asked, a little alarmed.

He nodded. "Everything is fine."

Nicoletti relaxed. "That's good."

The Doctor looked at her. "Lieutenant Nicoletti . . . are you a virgin?"

She felt her cheeks flushing. "I beg your pardon?"

"A virgin," he repeated. "Someone who has yet to—"

"I know what it *means,*" she told him. "I just don't know what it has to do with my virus."

"Oh," the Doctor said, "it has nothing to do with it. In fact, there's no longer any trace of the virus in your system."

"In that case, it's none of your business, Doctor" said Nicoletti, swinging her legs out of bed, "and I think I'll report to engineering."

"You don't understand," the Doctor protested. "This is not a matter of simple curiosity."

"It's still none of your business," she muttered. Then she made her way out of sickbay by the quickest route possible.

* * *

The Doctor approached the holodeck, still a little embarassed by his exchange with Lieutenant Nicoletti. His function on *Voyager* was to heal people, not send them flying out of sickbay.

Still, his intentions had been honorable. In the course of his survey of various holidays, one on the planet Tiraccus III had caught his eye. In ancient times, it had involved the ritual sacrifice of a virgin on a slab of newly cut obsidian.

In modern times, a virgin was still required, but his or her sacrifice was only conducted on a symbolic level. One might say many things about the Tiraccans, but at least they hadn't let the march of progress pass them by.

In any case, the Doctor's experience with the lieutenant had led him to consider another holiday.

"Computer," said the Doctor. "Initiate Wedding of Rixx program, complete with recent modifications."

A moment later, the interlocking doors slid away and revealed the fruits of the Doctor's labors. He stepped inside the holodeck and looked around.

Very nice, he thought. Very nice indeed. And as anyone who knew him could attest, he was notoriously difficult to please.

The room in which he found himself was expansive, with a high vaulted ceiling and a columnlike structure in each corner. It was lit in a way that gave the walls a mellow, golden glow.

The wall hangings were free-form, comprised of burnished metals in a great variety of pleasing shapes and sizes. The furniture was made up of velvet divans and satin love seats presented in a half-dozen pastel hues, the floor an intriguing pattern of light and dark tiles.

"Stately," the Doctor said out loud. "Even regal." But then, as a guest of the Fifth House of Betazed, he had expected no less.

He looked out his window at the elaborate white marble stair that connected the sprawling lower lawn with the even more sprawling upper lawn. The rails on either side of it, also cut from white marble, were festooned with garlands of dark blue and blood-red uttaberry blossoms.

Beyond the stair, between two towering trees with silver leaves, a white canopy shot through with thread-of-latinum had been elevated on yellow-and-white striped poles. The sun filtered through the canopy, glinting off the ancient silver chalice that graced a marble stand within.

The Sacred Chalice of Rixx, the Doctor noted with some satisfaction.

It was one of the most valuable artifacts on Betazed, and had been for the last seven hundred years. The chalice was brought out only once a year, in recognition of the emperor Rixx's mythical marriage to the goddess Niiope.

In the twenty-fourth century, Betazoids no longer worshipped gods and goddesses, of course. However, they were still eager to celebrate the holidays associated with said gods and goddesses—particularly *this* one.

The Wedding of Rixx, he thought excitedly, was the most important celebration on the entire planet, observed by young and old alike. Indeed, it was one of the most festive occasions anywhere in the galaxy.

Never having set foot on any planet in the Alpha Quadrant, where Betazed happened to be located, the Doctor couldn't know this from personal experience. However, *Voyager*'s computer had given a wealth of information on the subject. In fact, he had perused only a fraction of it, preferring to be surprised and delighted by the experience.

Just then, he heard the strident tinkling of Betazoid cymbals. Their purpose was to alert all and sundry that the ceremony would begin in five minutes. The Doctor smiled with anticipation.

Now, he thought, all I need are some appropriate garments. However, he couldn't see anything even vaguely resembling a closet in the room. His first impulse was to ask the computer for an explanation—but in the end, he decided against it.

When on Betazed, he mused, do as the Betazoids do. Spotting what looked like a set of wind chimes near a particularly elegant divan, he crossed the room and tapped them with his finger.

Surprisingly, the sounds that came from them were nearly as strident as those made by the cymbals a moment earlier. However, they had an almost immediate effect, as the Doctor heard footfalls approaching from outside the room. Before long, there was a knock on the door.

"Come in," he said.

The door opened and a female attendant entered the room. She had long red hair and a rather pleasing appearance.

"How may I assist you?" she asked the Doctor.

"I need some clothing appropriate for the celebration," he told her. He indicated his black-and-blue

Starfleet uniform. "Obviously, I can't attend in this old thing."

The Betazoid looked at him as if he had suggested she lay an egg in the center of the room. Then she smiled. "You're joking, aren't you?"

The Doctor returned her gaze. "That wasn't my intention. Just what is it about my request you find humorous?"

The attendant didn't answer right away. She seemed to be searching for the right words. But before she could find any, the Doctor saw something attract her attention.

Something seen through the window, he thought. Frowning, he turned and took a look in the same direction.

Suddenly, no explanation was necessary. The Doctor approached the window and leaned on the sill, his gaze fixed on the procession of thoroughly *naked* Betazoids marching across the lower lawn.

Naked, he repeated silently for emphasis.

No clothes.

None at all.

As he watched, the procession reached the stair and ascended it, then headed for the wedding canopy. The Betazoids chatted and laughed and clasped their hands with joy. None of them seemed to feel the least bit self-conscious about their nakedness.

The Doctor tried to picture himself in the midst of the celebrants—and shuddered. As a physician, he had been trained to view the humanoid form dispassionately, even clinically—but not when that form was his own.

Perhaps it was a glitch in his programming, or an

idiosyncrasy derived from one of the physician-personalities he was modeled after. The Doctor didn't really know where his sense of modesty came from.

He was certain of only one thing—he very much did *not* wish to traipse around without clothes in public. Ergo, he would have to forgo any participation in the Wedding of Rixx.

Sighing, the Doctor turned away from the window—and realized that his attendant was still present. She smiled at him again.

"That's a very nice shade of red," she told him.

His hand flew to his face. "I do *not* turn red," he insisted.

"Er . . . of course not," the Betazoid replied.

"You may go," the Doctor told her.

She started to leave, then stopped and turned to look at him. "If you hurry," she said, "you can still make the ceremony."

"Thank you," he said, "but I don't think I'll be attending this year." He looked up at the ceiling. "Computer, end program."

A moment later, the Doctor was standing in an empty holodeck. Glancing over his shoulder, he saw that the naked Betazoids were gone—and with them, any possibility of his becoming naked and joining them.

Oh well, he thought, pulling down his uniform front with a sense of propriety. Back to the proverbial drawing board.

As Janeway emerged from the turbolift onto *Voyager*'s bridge, she took in the image on the forward viewscreen. It was just as Chakotay had described it to her.

Three ships were hanging motionless in space. With the exception of a minor detail here and there, they were almost identical to one another. They also bore a strong resemblance to the Caatati vessel *Voyager* had encountered days earlier.

"They're in bad shape," Chakotay told her, joining her as she took up a position by her center seat.

"How bad?" the captain asked.

"As bad as Rahmin's ship," the first officer told her. "Maybe worse."

Janeway glanced at Tuvok, then Ensign Kim. Their grim expressions only confirmed Chakotay's report.

"The vessel in the center continues to hail us," the Vulcan noted for the captain's benefit.

"Open a channel," Janeway told him. "On screen."

A somber visage appeared on the viewer. As the captain had expected, he was a Caatati. And he was every bit as pale and emaciated and hollow-eyed as Rahmin had been. No, Janeway thought—even *more* so.

She suppressed a sigh and identified herself. "I'm Captain Kathryn Janeway of the Federation starship *Voyager*."

"Yes," said the Caatati, "I know. My name is Lumas. I'm in charge of my vessel as well as the two that accompany it."

"You've spoken recently with Rahmin," the captain deduced.

"I have been in contact with him," Lumas admitted. "While we Caatati don't usually travel as a group,

145

we still communicate from time to time." He paused, as if seeking a way to phrase his thoughts. "Rahmin told us of your great generosity."

"He needed help," Janeway responded succinctly. "We did whatever we could for him."

Lumas looked like a hungry man forced to watch as someone else ate. "Captain," he ventured, "would it be possible for me to have a word with you? In private, perhaps?"

Janeway glanced at Chakotay. He shrugged, indicating he had no objection to the idea. Tuvok was another matter.

"Captain," he said, "I must advise you—"

"I know," she replied. "And thank you, Lieutenant."

Despite the Vulcan's warning, she wasn't particularly wary of Lumas and his ships. After all, Rahmin's Caatati had been just what they claimed to be— refugees from a Borg attack. According to *Voyager's* sensor scans, Lumas's group was in much the same straits.

Of course, the captain had an inkling of how her conversation with Lumas might go. But that didn't deter her in the least.

"If you lower your shields," she told the Caatati, "I'll have my transporter operator bring you aboard."

Lumas's brow wrinkled. "Transporter . . . ?" he asked.

Janeway smiled a sober smile. "Trust me. It'll be easier to explain once you're here."

The Caatati smiled back as best he could. Then he turned to some offscreen technican and gave an order. A moment later, Lumas returned his attention to the captain.

"Our shields are down," he said. "That is, what's left of them."

Janeway nodded. "Transporter room one. Lock on to the coordinates of the Cataati with whom I've been speaking and beam him aboard."

"Aye, Captain," came the response from the transporter room.

Janeway glanced at Tuvok. "See to it our friend Lumas is escorted to the briefing room. And ask Mr. Neelix to join us there as well. He knows our food supplies better than anyone."

"Acknowledged," said the Vulcan.

The captain turned to the viewscreen again. After a moment or two, Lumas was surrounded by the shimmering aura of the transporter effect. Then he vanished from the screen altogether.

Janeway heaved a sigh. This wasn't going to be easy. She could cope with subspace anomalies and hostile life-forms. But a people who needed more help than she could give?

That was a different story entirely.

CHAPTER

11

THE DOCTOR STOOD IN A DRY RIVERBED IN THE MIDDLE OF the Phaelonian Wasteland and gazed at the native Phaelonians amassed all around him.

Tall, graceful beings with golden eyes and scaly, purple skin, they wore black breeches, shirts, and headbands to commemorate their holiday, the Vernal Processional. Having had his fill of costuming traditions after his Betazoid experience, the Doctor wore his uniform instead.

Thanks to some tinkering he had done with the program, no one noticed that he was dressed any differently. For that matter, no one noticed that he was a human instead of a Phaelonian. That was one of the advantages of a holographic simulation—one could diverge from the norm and get away with it.

Most of the Doctor's fellow observers were gazing upriver, the direction from which the processional was to arrive. They seemed excited by the prospect, despite the oppressive waves of heat that rose from the riverbed.

The Doctor admitted that he was excited, too. The thought of a parade appealed to him. No doubt, it would have its share of well-dressed Phaelonians and festively decorated carriages. Maybe even a juggler.

After all, this event was an important one to the Phaelonians. In ancient times, it was considered an inducement for the gods to flood the riverbed with snowmelt from nearby mountains—and, in the process, make fertile the land all around it.

As with so many other holidays, it had outlived its original intent. However, one couldn't deny its prominence in Phaelonian arts and culture. There were, for instance, some seventy-two metaphors in the local tongue that focused on the processional, though the Doctor had bothered to read only a couple of them.

In fact, he had done in this case pretty much what he had done in his study of the Wedding of Rixx. In other words, very little—even though, in the Betazoid program, the Doctor's minimal scholarship had proven his undoing.

But how could he judge the full value of a celebration if he knew in advance everything that would happen? How could he be spontaneous? Indeed, how could he have a good time?

Turning to a Phaelonian who seemed even more eager than the others, the Doctor said, "It should be a good one this year."

It was an innocuous enough remark, he thought. And yet, it was calculated to initiate a conversation.

The Phaelonian smiled. "It depends on the *abendaar.*"

Ah yes, thought the Doctor. The *abendaar*—a Phaelonian beast of burden. He had learned that much, at least.

Long ago, *abendaar* had pulled the Phaelonians' carts and carriages. It was only logical that they would figure prominently in a ceremonial march.

"I take it you've done this before?" the Doctor asked.

"Once," the Phaelonian told him. "My sibling did it three times."

"Oh?" said the Doctor. "Is he here?"

The Phaelonian's enthusiasm seemed to dim a bit. "No, though I wish he were. No one enjoyed the processional as much as he did."

"Too bad," the Doctor remarked sympathetically. "Maybe he'll be able to make it next year."

The Phaelonian looked at him, but didn't answer. And a moment later, he moved away.

An odd response, the Doctor mused. Perhaps I *should* have studied local customs a bit more thoroughly.

Looking about, he noticed a change in his companions' behavior. Many of them were bending over, stretching their limbs this way and that. A few even went so far as to help each other.

Rather than appear iconoclastic, the Doctor began to stretch as well. Still, he felt a little foolish. After all, how limber did one have to be to appreciate a parade?

Then the Phaelonians stopped stretching. But they seemed edgy, the Doctor thought, taut with anticipation. His curiosity got the better of him.

"Why is everyone so jumpy?" he asked one of them.

The Phaelonian laughed grimly. "As if you didn't know."

"In fact," he said, "I don't know."

But that Phaelonian didn't seem to believe him. No doubt the Doctor's native appearance had something to do with that.

Then the Doctor heard it. It started as a subtle rhythm in the ground beneath his feet. Then it got stronger, more insistent.

The Doctor looked around. "What is that?"

The Phaelonians on every side of him were still looking upriver. But now, one by one, they seemed to be bracing themselves in the manner of sprinters preparing for a race.

"Won't somebody tell me what's going on?" the Doctor entreated.

By then, the rhythm in the ground had become forceful enough to make his bones shudder. And soon it was more than a rhythm—it was a sound.

A sound of thunder.

As the Doctor watched, spellbound, a cloud of dust rose from somewhere upriver. Something was stirring it up, he concluded. He couldn't imagine what that something might be.

Or for that matter, how it would effect the processional.

"There!" yelled a Phaelonian, pointing to the cloud.

No, the Doctor realized. Not the cloud itself, but the mass of muscular black flesh and ruby-red eyes that was emerging from it.

The *abendaar* were coming, all right. But not in a neat parade, drawing well-dressed Phaelonians in festively decorated coaches. They were coming in a wild and untamed horde.

And they were advancing on the Doctor and his companions with the speed of summer lightning.

Suddenly, he understood. The Phaelonians hadn't gathered in the river bed to act as spectators. They had come here to race the *abendaar* from some prearranged point to some other point, presumably one of safety.

But in the process, they would be risking their lives against what amounted to a prodigiously powerful force of nature.

It was insane. It went against the entire complex of instincts that had enabled the Phaelonians to survive their evolution into sentient beings. And yet, in some ways, it was a classic sacrifice, offering up existing life in the hope the land would make new life possible.

Of course, the Doctor was tempted to put an end to the program then and there. He had no desire to suffer the indignity of being trampled by large, smelly beasts—or to watch his fellow celebrants become smears on the granular surface of the riverbed.

But he reminded himself of why he had initiated the program in the first place. He was seeking a particular kind of experience—and here it was, in all its primal splendor.

If he shut it down, he would never know what he had missed. So against his better judgment, he hunkered down like all the other Phaelonians and waited while the *abendaar* bore down on them.

The sound in the ground grew louder and louder still, loud enough to rattle the Doctor's holographic bones. But no one else was moving, so he didn't either. He just watched the darting eyes and tensing muscles of the Phaelonians and braced himself for the race's start.

In the event, there was no signal the Doctor could discern—no cry of encouragement, no starting gun. The Phaelonians didn't seem to need one. They simply surged forward as one.

The Doctor started forward, too. But right from the beginning, he was a step behind them. With their natural grace and long strides, the Phaelonians soon widened that gap from one step to two and then three.

The *abendaar,* meanwhile, were flooding the dry channel like a dark and malevolent riptide, tossing their triangular, tufted heads and beating the sand with their rock-hard hooves. The Doctor spared only a glance at them, but the sight wasn't encouraging.

He ran as hard as he could, his arms pumping, his feet digging into the riverbed with all the rapidity he could muster. But as fast as the Doctor raced, as hard as he pushed himself, it was clearly not fast enough. The beasts behind him were gaining on him at an alarming rate, while the Phaelonians were gradually leaving him behind.

Come on, the Doctor urged himself. Accelerate. Get a move on, you laggard.

But he couldn't. In fact, it became more and more difficult merely to maintain the same pace. His physical limitations, never an issue before, were suddenly and shockingly brought to the fore.

This was a new experience for him, and not a very

pleasant one. The Doctor would have stopped altogether but for his determination to complete the holiday experience.

The snorting and pounding behind him was increasingly audible. Wretched animals, he thought. Didn't they have anything better to do with their time than run down the premiere physician in the quadrant?

Gradually, the Doctor felt himself faltering. Slowing down, despite his desire to the contrary.

The *abendaar,* however, showed no signs of sympathy. If anything, their eyes seemed to get wilder, their chomping more furious, the roar of their progress ever more deafening.

The heat, meanwhile, was intense, almost tangible. It attacked him from within and without, seeming to rob him of energy.

As he plumbed himself for some reserve he hadn't yet tapped, he made a mental note to add more stamina to his program.

Thinking this, distracted by it, the Doctor stumbled—and nearly pitched forward in the riverbed. But somehow, he caught himself and kept on.

How much longer could this go on? he wondered. How much longer could he push his holographic form to its limits?

Then the Doctor saw them. Up ahead, in the distance. Two crowds of Phaelonians, one on each side of the riverbed.

Unlike the runners, these people were dressed all in white. And some of them were kneeling along the banks, as if they wished to get as intimate with the action as possible.

By then, the Doctor was nine or ten strides behind even the slowest of the Phaelonian sprinters, and as many as fifteen behind the quickest. But he could see the leaders splitting off to one side of the riverbed or the other.

As they approached the crowds, those who were kneeling knelt even lower. Then they stretched their arms out toward the runners.

Abruptly, the Doctor figured out their intent. The white-garbed Phaelonians were going to lift their black-garbed brethren out of harm's way.

That is, he added, if they made it there in time.

At the moment, it looked as if every one of the native racers would do that. The lone exception was the Doctor himself.

Once more, he allowed himself a glance at the beasts pursuing him. Immediately, he wished he hadn't. They were even closer than he had imagined—fifty meters at best—and they were getting closer with each thunderous beat of their hooves.

Facing forward again, he set his sights on his potential saviors. As the first of the runners reached them, he was swept up out of the riverbed and embraced by the crowd. On the other side, another runner was pulled out of harm's way. And another.

The sprinters seemed exhilarated—intoxicated with their triumph. The Doctor longed to feel the same thrill, but he had a long way to go.

The *abendaar* behind him grunted and whined in their attempts to overtake him. He could smell their musky odor. He could even feel their hot breath on his neck.

Up ahead, most of the other runners had finished

their race, and the crowds on the banks were plucking more of them out of the channel every second. Only a handful of stragglers remained.

And even *they* had a lead on the Doctor.

He lifted his chin and thrust out his chest. Then he poured everything he had into one last, magnificent effort.

It wasn't enough. Fewer than thirty meters from salvation, the Doctor felt something hit him from behind. Sprawling forward, he cried out in instinctive panic. "Computer—terminate program!"

The next thing he knew, he was standing in an empty holodeck. The *abendaar* were gone. So were the Phaelonians.

He had failed to finish the program, he noted with regret. Or, perhaps more accurately, the program had succeeded in finishing him. And yet, he had been so close . . .

Disgruntled, disappointed, the Doctor exited the holodeck. Yet another holiday experience had proven troublesome for him. Clearly, he told himself as he emerged into the corridor, he would have to rethink his approach.

CHAPTER
12

JANEWAY SAT ACROSS THE BRIEFING ROOM TABLE FROM Lumas, flanked by Neelix and Tuvok. All she could think of was that the Caatati looked worse in person than on *Voyager*'s viewscreen.

"Your transporter technology is amazing," Lumas told her.

"Only if you've never seen it before," the captain assured him. "But then," she said gently, "you didn't ask to see me to discuss technology."

The Caatati smiled a wan smile. "No," he agreed. "I didn't." He lowered his eyes, as if he had suddenly found some interesting detail in the surface of the table. "It is not easy for me to speak of this, Captain Janeway."

"Which is why you wished to speak in private," said the captain. "I understand."

Lumas took a breath and let it out. "There are over

two hundred people on our three ships alone," he began. "Every one of them suffers from malnourishment, to one degree or another."

"It must be difficult," Neelix observed.

"It is," said the Caatati. "But it's been hardest on the children. Every parent sacrifices for his or her child, but even so, there's not enough food. If you could hear the crying of the babies . . ." He shook his head. "You would have as much trouble sleeping at night as I do."

"Have you considered relocation to a planet?" asked Tuvok. "One, perhaps, where you could grow your own food?"

Lumas gave him a withering look. "You speak as though such planets are easily found, Lieutenant. Believe me, they're not. And those that exist have already been claimed."

"Perhaps their occupants would be willing to share their resources with you," the Vulcan suggested reasonably. "In the same way that we shared our resources with Rahmin."

"You'd be surprised," said Lumas, "to find how unwelcome people can be when they've fallen on hard times. Because we have nothing of value, we're treated like vagrants . . . even criminals."

"We're not unsympathetic," Janeway told him. "But *Voyager* isn't an entire planet—it's just a ship. We have limited supplies. We can't possibly provide enough for all your people."

Lumas looked around at the briefing room. He ran his fingers over the flawless surface of the table.

"Forgive me," he said, "but from my perspective, Captain, you live in the midst of luxury. You don't suffer from debilitating diseases. You have many energy sources, not to mention transporters and replicators. And your crew is wellfed." The Cataati leaned forward. "Apparently, keeping your bellies full is more important to you than helping those less fortunate."

Suddenly, his tone had become bitter. His mild-mannered request had become an accusation. Janeway found she didn't care for the transformation.

"Wait just a second," Neelix interjected. "That's decidedly unfair. Captain Janeway is the most generous person you could ever hope to meet." He held his hands out in an appeal for reason. "But if we were to give supplies to everyone who asked . . . we wouldn't have anything left."

Lumas's anger seemed to drain away. He shook his head in despair. "Of course not," he agreed. "It was unfair of me to suggest otherwise. You're just trying to survive . . . as we are."

Janeway frowned. Then she turned to her chief cook and morale officer. "Neelix, how much food can we spare?"

The Talaxian shrugged. "We could provide each ship with several hundred kilograms. It would alleviate their problem for a while, at least."

"Arrange for transport," the captain ordered. "And check with the doctor to see if he can spare any medical supplies."

Neelix nodded. "Aye, Captain."

Lumas laid his ridged forehead against the briefing room table. He seemed overwhelmed with gratitude.

"Thank you," he told Janeway. He lifted his head

again. "May the gods smile on you and your crew. Tonight, our starving children will go to sleep without hunger. When they ask, I will tell them it is because of the generosity of the captain of *Voyager*."

Janeway wished she could feel good about Lumas's gratitude. Unfortunately, she didn't. In fact, if she didn't know better, she would have felt she was being used.

After all, Tuvok had had a point. As the captain's father had often pointed out to her, Providence helped those who helped themselves.

"I urge you to keep looking for a homeworld," she told the Cataati. "One that might support you and your people. We want all those children to grow up strong and healthy."

"Perhaps now they will," Lumas replied.

Janeway turned to her tactical officer. "Tuvok, please escort our guest back to the transporter room."

Lumas got up and approached the captain. Taking her hand, he squeezed it in a final gesture of gratitude. Then he followed the Vulcan out of the room.

Janeway sat back in her seat and looked at Neelix. The Talaxian didn't seem any more gratified than she did.

"Well," he said, "I guess I'll see about those supplies."

But he didn't go anywhere. Obviously, there was something on his mind.

"What is it?" the captain asked.

Neelix's brow furrowed. "Rahmin said there were nearly *thirty* of these ships. What happens when we run into the next bunch? And the next? What do we tell *them?*"

The captain didn't have an answer—because there wasn't one. She put her hand on the Talaxian's shoulder. "I guess we'll just have to cross that bridge when we come to it."

The Doctor glanced around the table and smiled at each of the seven people seated about it.

The children, Naomi, Benjamin, and Aaron, smiled back at him. So did Lt. Rabinowitz and his sister and brother-in-law, Carla and David Sokolov. Only the elderly Aunt Pearl gave him less than a hearty acknowledgment.

Lt. Rabinowitz, who was seated on the Doctor's left, leaned closer to him. "It's not you," he said. "It's her gall bladder. It always acts up this time of year."

The Doctor nodded politely. "I see," he responded, though he was at a loss as to why such an ailment might manifest itself on a seasonal basis. He was still considering the problem when David picked up his padd and cleared his throat.

"Shall we begin?" he asked.

"Isn't that why we're here?" Aunt Pearl answered drily.

David smiled at her. "So it is."

With one hand, he indicated the glass of wine set before him. In fact, all the people present had glasses of something set before them—wine in the case of the adults, grape juice in the case of the children.

With the other hand, David held up his padd. "Baruch attah adonai, elohainu melech haolahm, borai p'ree hagahfen. Blessed art Thou, O Eternal, our God, King of the Universe, Creator of the fruit of the vine."

"You needn't translate for my benefit," the Doctor assured him. "I'm quite conversant in a variety of Terran languages and dialects."

David glanced at him. "Thank you for sharing that, but we always say the prayers in both Hebrew and English. It's sort of a tradition in our family, going back some four hundred years."

"Ah," the Doctor replied. "I see. In that case, please proceed."

His host did just that—almost as if he were the real David Sokolov and not a holographic recreation of the lieutenant's brother-in-law. "Baruch attah adonai, elohainu melech haolahm, shehecheyanu v'kee-yamanu v'heegeeyanu lazmahn hazeh. Blessed art Thou, O Eternal, our God, King of the Universe, who has preserved us, sustained us, and allowed us to enjoy this season."

With that, David picked up his glass and drank from it. Looking around, the Doctor saw that everyone else was following suit. Lifting his own glass, he inhaled its bouquet for a moment, then sipped at it.

"Chateau Picard '64," he noted. "An excellent year."

Carla darted a glance at her husband. "I'm glad *someone* around here appreciates fine wine."

Lt. Rabinowitz chuckled. "An old debate. I'm sorry you stumbled on it, Doctor."

The Doctor looked around the table. "Well, it *is* a fine wine."

"*Thank* you," Carla said pointedly.

David shot them both a look of forced tolerance, then returned his attention to his padd. "I will now wash my hands."

"Always a good idea," the Doctor remarked. "As they say, cleanliness is next to godliness."

"Who says that?" asked Aaron, the youngest child. He eyed the Doctor with undisguised skepticism.

"Never mind," his mother told him. "Just pay attention."

Ignoring the exchange, David cleansed his hands in a small bowl apparently reserved for the purpose. Then he said another prayer—this one over a small bundle of parsley, which he dipped in a second bowl and distributed to everyone at the table.

Seeing Lt. Rabinowitz munch on his sprig of parsley, the Doctor did likewise. He found it salty, and since parsley was not salty in and of itself, he gathered that the water in the bowl had contained salt.

"It represents the tears of the Israelites," Lt. Rabinowitz pointed out to him. "Because of the oppression they suffered in Egypt."

The Doctor nodded. "Thank you. You're being very helpful."

"No problem," said Rabinowitz.

The Doctor congratulated himself on his strategy. With the lieutenant as a guide, he would no doubt avoid the problems he had encountered in his previous holiday scenarios—while preserving the potential for surprise and spontaneity.

As it happened, Rabinowitz had been eager to relive this holiday meal—a celebration of the ancient Jewish feast of Passover. He had even offered to set up the program parameters, obviating the need for the Doctor to conduct any further research.

After all, the lieutenant had been exploring the Delta Quadrant for the last few years, along with the rest of *Voyager*'s crew. He hadn't seen his sister and her family in quite some time—and unless the captain found a way to accelerate their journey home, he would never see them again.

Except *this* way, of course. In a holodeck setting, where Rabinowitz could make his most poignant memories manifest.

"It's too hot in here," Aunt Pearl said suddenly. "Somebody open a window or something."

"It's too soon for Elijah," Benjamin piped up.

The Doctor looked to his "guide" for an explanation. Rabinowitz chuckled and mussed Benjamin's hair.

"Elijah was a prophet," he told the Doctor. "He represents the needy—the stranger. Later on, after we finish eating, we open the door for him so he can come in and share our food."

"Of course," said the Doctor. "Much as the Caatati have been given a portion of *Voyager*'s resources."

"Actually," the lieutenant told him, "that's not a bad analogy."

As David opened a window for Aunt Pearl, Carla was doing something with a stack of crumbly-looking flatbreads on a plate near the center of the table. The Doctor craned his neck in order to watch.

"Matzoth," explained Rabinowitz. "Pieces of un-leavened bread—like those baked in a hurry by the Israelites as they left Egypt. Carla's breaking the middle piece in half for a kids' game that'll happen later."

David sat down again. Then the lieutenant's sister elevated the plate of matzoth and read from her own padd.

"This is the bread of affliction which our ancestors ate in the land of Egypt. Let all those who are hungry come in and eat. Let all those who are in distress come in and celebrate the Passover. This year, we celebrate here, but next year we hope to celebrate in the land of Israel. This year, we are slaves; next year, may we be free men."

The Doctor didn't understand everything Carla had said. He turned to Rabinowitz for an explanation—and was surprised to see tears standing in the lieutenant's eyes.

"Sorry," said Rabinowitz. He smiled. "It's just that I've been away for a long time and I miss them."

The Doctor nodded. "As you should. You have a fine family." He gave the lieutenant a moment to compose himself. "If you don't mind, I have a question."

"Ask away," Rabinowitz told him. "Answering questions is what the seder is all about."

"I heard your sister speak of the bread of affliction—clearly, a reference to the matzoth she was holding up."

"That's right," said the lieutenant.

"And she expressed the ethic of charity which you mentioned in connection with the prophet Elijah."

"Right again."

"But," the Doctor noted, "she spoke of a wish to be in the land of Israel, though—as you told me—she and her family live in North America. Also, she referred to herself as a slave . . . ?"

"When she appears to enjoy the same freedoms as any other Federation citizen."

The Doctor nodded. "Exactly."

Rabinowitz picked up the padd in front of him and tapped in a command. Then he read out loud.

"In every generation, each individual is bound to regard himself as if he himself had gone out of Egypt. As it is said, 'And thou shalt relate to thy son this very day, this is what the Lord did for me when I left Egypt.' Thus, it was not our ancestors alone who were redeemed, but us as well."

"Hey, Unk—no skipping ahead," Naomi insisted.

"Sorry," said the lieutenant, feigning contrition. Then he turned to the Doctor. "You see? In a sense, we *are* slaves, just like our ancestors. And just like them, we yearn to leave Egypt and be free."

The Doctor looked at him. "So . . . you're asserting a bond of kinship with those who came before you."

"Actually," Rabinowitz told him, "it's more than that. We're saying, in a literal way, that we are the people the Pharaohs enslaved in Egypt—and that those people are us."

The Doctor thought about that for a moment. Obviously, this was a rather considerable leap of faith.

"What if one doesn't feel that way?" he asked. "What if one merely sees the liberation from Egypt as an intriguing historical event?"

Rabinowitz looked at him with a touch of sadness in his eyes. "One would still be welcome at the seder, Doctor."

The Doctor felt as if he had lost something important. "Thank you," he told the lieutenant.

"Glad to be of service," said Rabinowitz.

CHAPTER
13

PARIS TRIED TO IGNORE THE STARES HE AND HIS COMPANION were getting as they negotiated one of *Voyager's* corridors. Apparently, people still weren't used to the idea of a Borg with the run of the ship.

"I've never navigated a transwarp conduit," he told Seven of Nine. "Any problems I should be aware of?"

She gave him an imperious glance. "You'll have no idea what you're doing. If we attempt to enter a transwarp conduit, I will have to take conn control. Any other course would be foolish."

Paris shrugged good-naturedly. "I *am* a quick study."

But the Borg was persistent. "There will be a number of gravimetric instabilities in the conduit. If they're not handled in precisely the right manner, the ship will be torn apart."

Paris chuckled. I can be persistent, too, he thought.

"Just out of curiosity, I'd like to take a look at the field displacement parameters. Could you set them for me?"

Seven of Nine glanced at him. "They will be of no use to you."

"Even so," he said, turning on the charm.

The Borg frowned ever so slightly. "All right."

There, the helmsman thought. We're having a conversation. A *productive* conversation. This isn't nearly as difficult as I thought it might be.

Of course, from the moment Seven of Nine had been disconnected from the Borg collective, Paris had had less trouble accepting her than some of his crewmates. He had been inclined to treat her as a person, not someone who might try to assimilate him at the drop of a nanite probe.

There was a corner up ahead. As they approached it, Paris tried to think of what other data he might need from Seven of Nine.

The flight controller was still thinking when he and the Borg made their turn—and saw two people walking in the opposite direction. One was Lieutenant Tuvok. The other was a Caatati.

Paris wasn't surprised to see the visitor. He hadn't been present on the bridge when *Voyager* encountered the Caatati ships, but word spread quickly on a starship.

Then Paris remembered who was with him. Seven of Nine, whose collective had assimilated most of the Caatati and all but destroyed their civilization. This could be trouble, he told himself.

For a moment, the alien didn't seem to realize what he was looking at. Then he stopped in the middle of his sentence and stared at the Borg with increasing intensity.

"What species is that?" he asked Tuvok.

By then, the Vulcan must have known there was no way to defuse the situation. But to his credit, he still tried.

"Her name is Seven of Nine," he replied reluctantly. "She is a human who lived as a Borg."

Suddenly, the alien's expression changed. His face twisted with hatred and loathing. Stopping dead in his tracks, he raised a bony hand and pointed a spindly finger at Seven of Nine.

"Borg!" he grated.

Seven of Nine returned the alien's scrutiny, but she said nothing.

"Do not be alarmed," Tuvok advised his companion. "She is disconnected from the Borg collective. She won't harm you."

But the Caatati seemed to have other problems with the Borg's presence. "Where's my wife?" he demanded raggedly, advancing on Seven of Nine. "Where are my children?" His voice became shrill and tremulous. "What did you do with them after you took them?"

Without warning, the alien lunged at Seven of Nine. By then, he was shrieking like a banshee, filling the corridor with his cries.

"What have you done with my family, you vicious predator? Give them back, do you hear? I want them back!"

Tuvok grabbed the Caatati by the waist and pulled him back. At the same time, Paris stepped protectively in front of Seven of Nine.

He doubted that the Borg was in any real danger. She seemed more than capable of taking care of herself, especially against someone as feeble as the alien. But Seven of Nine was a guest on *Voyager,* and he wasn't going to allow her to be manhandled by another guest.

"Mr. Paris," said the Vulcan, "please proceed." Then he ushered the Cataati down the corridor.

"You don't have to tell me twice," Paris muttered.

Taking the Borg's arm, he guided her in the opposite direction and didn't look back. It was a while before the echoes of the alien's venom faded with distance.

The flight controller turned to Seven of Nine. "Sorry about that."

"About what?" she asked.

"Well," said Paris, "the way he reacted to you."

The Borg seemed puzzled. The concern he was showing was obviously beyond her range of understanding.

"He didn't injure me," she pointed out.

He nodded. "Good."

For a moment, they walked in silence, Paris glancing at Seven of Nine only once or twice. Then she spoke up again.

"There are many on this ship who have similar feelings toward me," she observed, "though I will admit I don't fully understand the reasons for their resentment." She turned to him, as if for affirmation.

He sighed, reluctant to lie to her. "I'm afraid you're right. I guess some people are having a harder time than others adjusting to the idea of a Borg on the ship.

They see you and they think of destruction and assimilation."

Seven of Nine tilted her head slightly. "Hence, the resentment."

"That's right." Paris studied her features. "Does that bother you? The way they feel, I mean?"

The Borg went silent again for a moment. "No," she said at last. "It doesn't."

He continued to study her. "I just want you to know I'm not one of those people—the ones who resent you. I mean, we all have a past we're not proud of." The flight controller rethought the sentiment. "Well, maybe not all of us, but *I* certainly do."

Seven of Nine didn't ask what he had done. Still, Paris had the feeling she wanted to know.

"A while back," he said, "I accidentally caused the death of a colleague. Worse, I lied about it. In the end, I disgraced my family and myself. I became a mercenary, a dead-ender without principles—willing to fight for anyone who would pay my bar bills."

He looked into the Borg's eyes. "But none of that matters anymore—not what I did, not what you did. What matters is what we say and do *now.*"

Seven of Nine tilted her head slightly. "I am uncertain of what you're attempting to say."

Paris tried to explain. "That . . . if there's any way I can help you adjust to life on *Voyager* . . . please ask me."

The Borg cast a sidelong look at him. She seemed cautious, even wary. But then, she barely knew him—barely knew anyone on *Voyager.* In her place, in a strange environment, he would have been uncertain about the motives of everyone around him.

But Paris was sincere in his desire to help her. He hoped Seven of Nine knew that.

"I will remember your offer," she told him.

A moment later, they reached engineering.

Tuvok guided Lumas along the corridor as gently as he could. The Caatati seemed stunned by his encounter with Seven of Nine, as if he had been dealt an actual, physical blow.

"She's a Borg," Lumas spat, and not for the first time. "A Borg . . ."

When they entered the transporter room, Janeway was waiting for them with Burleson, the transporter operator. It didn't take the captain more than a glance to see that something was wrong.

The Caatati glowered at her. "How could you?" he gasped.

"How could I *what?*" asked Janeway.

"We encountered Seven of Nine in the corridor," the Vulcan explained, regretting the incident with an intensity no human would understand. "Our guest did not react positively to her presence."

Janeway nodded. "I see."

Lumas's mouth twisted with hatred. "She's a killer, Captain Janeway. She must be destroyed."

Janeway frowned. "She's not a killer anymore. She's been cut off from the Borg collective."

"No!" the Caatati insisted, his eyes blazing in their deep, shadowed sockets. "She'll betray you first chance she gets!"

"I'll take that into account," the captain said. Then she glanced at Tuvok. "If you please?"

The Vulcan took hold of Lumas's arm and escorted

him to the transporter grid. The Caatati struggled for a moment, but soon realized he had no chance against Tuvok's great strength.

"Don't be a fool!" Lumas rasped, remaining on the grid as the Vulcan stepped back. "Don't you know what the Borg are capable of? Kill her while you still can!"

Janeway didn't comment. Instead, she turned to the transporter operator. "Energize, Lieutenant."

Burleson did as she was told. The glittering transporter effect began to appear around the Caatati.

"Kill her!" Lumas insisted, his hands clenching into fists. "Make her pay for what she did! Make her—"

He was gone before he could get the rest out.

Tuvok looked at the captain. "I take full responsibility for what happened. I should have made certain of Seven of Nine's whereabouts before I escorted Lumas to the transporter room."

Janeway returned his gaze. "You're not perfect, Tuvok. No one is."

"I am the security officer on this ship," he pointed out. "Some oversights are inexcusable."

She sighed. "You'll do better next time."

"Indeed," said the Vulcan. "You may rely on that."

Changing the subject, the captain turned to the empty transporter grid. "You know," she remarked, "I liked it better when we were saying goodbye to Rahmin. He, at least, remembered to say thank you."

It was an unfortunate way to end their dealings with the Caatati, she mused. She just hoped it wouldn't come back to bite them in the end.

CHAPTER
14

When Janeway returned to her ready room, she found the Doctor waiting for her there.

"I hope you don't mind," he said. "I took the liberty of transferring my program to this location."

The captain frowned. "To be honest, Doctor, I'd prefer you didn't make a habit of it. A captain's ready room is her refuge. Her sanctum sanctorum, if you will. It's unsettling to come back to such a place and find someone else already there."

The Doctor nodded. "I understand. It won't happen again."

Janeway crossed the room and sat at her desk. "Thank you. But since you're here already, what can I do for you?"

"Are you . . . er, busy?" he asked.

"No more than unusual. What's on your mind?"

"I wish to . . . vent my frustrations," he said. "I

was hoping you wouldn't mind if I did it here. With you."

"Go ahead," she replied, though she had a feeling she might regret it.

The Doctor began to pace. "As you know, I've been sampling various holidays in an effort to find one to my liking."

"Yes," said the captain. "I know. Lieutenant Nicoletti is still wondering what you were up to."

The Doctor sighed. "An unfortunate incident. I made every attempt to explain my motivation to the lieutenant later on."

"I'm sure you did," Janeway told him, trying not to crack a smile. "In any case, you say you've been sampling various holidays . . ."

"But none of them appear to suit me. The Day of Honor ritual seemed barbaric and, frankly, a little disgusting as well. The Phaelonian holiday seemed unnecessarily rigorous. Also, I tend to shy away from leisure activities in which my life is at stake."

"Understandably," the captain noted.

"There was also the Betazoid holiday, which . . ." The Doctor glanced at her. "Which was inappropriate for other reasons."

"Didn't you attend a ceremony with Lt. Rabinowitz?"

"I did indeed," said the Doctor. "And, I must say, the lieutenant couldn't have been more helpful. However, I ultimately found that it. . . . did not relate to my personal experience."

"So you haven't had much luck," Janeway observed.

"That," said the Doctor, "would be putting it

mildly. Fortunately, I believe I see the problem now. In fact, it's something I probably should have seen a long time ago."

"And what's that?" Janeway asked him.

"One can't just embrace a holiday at random. A holiday is a cultural milestone—an event with which its celebrants have an intimate and long-standing relationship. And since I have no culture of my own, no heritage, it's impossible for me to ever feel part of such an event."

"I don't believe that," the captain responded. "Difficult, yes—but not impossible." She leaned forward. "Your problem, Doctor, is that you've been looking at the other man's grass."

He looked at her askance. "I beg your pardon?"

Janeway smiled. "The other man's grass. You know—the stuff that's always greener? In the old saw?"

"Ah," he said. "You mean I've valued other belief systems above my own."

"That's what I mean, all right."

"But," the Doctor complained, "I *have* no belief system. I only deal in those things that can be proven empirically."

"Not true," the captain insisted. "You believe in the value of friendship and family. You believe in courage and self-sacrifice—"

"The benefits of which are self-evident," he argued. "They can all be reduced to causes and effects. I mean a belief in something that *can't* be demonstrated or dissected—something that has no obvious benefits in the material world."

He was talking about a leap of faith. She said so.

The Doctor nodded. "A leap of faith."

Janeway regarded him. This wasn't going to be easy. On the other hand, she desperately didn't want to let the Doctor down.

After all, he had helped or comforted almost everyone who served on *Voyager* over the course of the last few years. The least she could do was provide *him* with some help and comfort.

And then it hit her.

"You know," the captain said, "you're right."

"About what? My having no belief system?" the Doctor asked.

"About a holiday being an event with which its celebrants have an intimate relationship—and a long-standing one. But you're *wrong* when you say you have no culture and no heritage. And you're even *more* wrong when you say you have no belief system."

He looked at her skeptically. "How so?"

"What do you do?" Janeway asked him.

The Doctor shrugged. "I'm a physician."

"A healer," she suggested.

"Yes . . ."

"And why do you do that? Because you have to? Because you're programmed to do so?"

The Doctor pondered the question. "I am programmed with certain knowledge—certain skills. But I act of my own volition. It would be inaccurate to say I heal people simply because my program calls for it."

"So you could choose *not* to heal them?"

He shrugged. "I suppose so, yes. But the context would have to be a rather bizarre one."

"Because life is sacred to you," Janeway suggested.

"One could say that, yes."

"And why is that?" she asked.

The Doctor grunted. "Surely you're joking."

"I'm not," the captain told him. "Why is life so sacred?"

He held his hands out. "Without life, the universe has no meaning."

"And what does the universe need with meaning, Doctor? Indeed," she pressed, "what difference does it make to the universe if any or all of your patients live or die?"

The Doctor looked about the room as if he thought he could find the answer floating in midair. After a while, he turned to her again, a bewildered expression on his face.

"Now that you mention it," he said, "it probably makes no difference at all."

Janeway smiled. "No difference. So life isn't so sacred after all?"

The Doctor did his best to understand the problem. "But it is. It *is* sacred."

"Despite all logic to the contrary? Despite the empirical evidence?"

"Despite that," he agreed.

The captain stood. "Then I suggest, Doctor, that you have made a leap of faith. What's more, you do it every day, without fail—just like every healer in the history of the universe, from the time of Hippocrates and even earlier."

He considered the possibility. "You're suggesting I'm part of some larger community after all. A community of physicians."

"That's right. And you don't wait for a holiday to

celebrate your faith. You do it all the time, morning, noon, and night."

The Doctor didn't speak for a long time. Then he said, "Perhaps you're right."

"You *know* I am," Janeway told him.

B'Elanna looked up from her console and saw Tom enter engineering with Seven of Nine. Deep inside, she felt a twinge. She was surprised to find that seeing the two of them together annoyed her.

Vorik, Carey, and the other engineers acknowledged Tom's presence with a nod. B'Elanna just turned back to her monitor.

Still, she couldn't help asking the question. "What brings you here, Tom?"

Paris glanced at her coolly. Obviously, he hadn't forgotten what they had said to each other in her quarters.

"I'm going to look at the field displacement parameters of the transwarp conduits. Seven's offered to establish them for me."

"How thoughtful," B'Elanna said.

He smiled a chilly smile. "I'm glad you approve."

"Actually," B'Elanna said, "I think we're ready to try opening one of the transwarp conduits—just as a test, of course."

"Great," Tom replied. "Let's give it a try."

By then, Seven of Nine had taken her place at her assigned workstation. "All systems are ready," she said flatly—even though no one had asked her for her assessment.

B'Elanna looked around. "All right. For now, we're

only going to take a peek. We'll open a conduit, get as much sensor data as we can, and then close it up again. I want to take this one step at a time—understood?"

Everyone nodded. Everyone except the Borg, of course, but she didn't seem to have any objection either.

Vorik spoke up. "I've set up a temporary tachyon matrix within the main deflector. It's on-line."

B'Elanna hit her commbadge. "Engineering to the bridge."

"Janeway here," came the response.

"We're ready to start, Captain."

"Go ahead, Lieutenant. We'll monitor your progress from here."

"Captain," said B'Elanna, "we'll have to be traveling at warp speed to create a large enough subspace field. I'd like permission to reroute conn control to engineering."

"Agreed," Janeway responded.

Turning to Tom, B'Elanna nodded. The flight controller went to a console and made the necessary adjustments. Seven of Nine watched him like a hawk the whole time. Eventually, Tom seemed to notice.

"Just for the purposes of this test," he assured the Borg.

Seven of Nine didn't answer. She just turned back to her own console.

B'Elanna didn't know what Tom was referring to, and right now she didn't care. She just wanted to get this over with.

"Mr. Paris?" she said.

Tom looked at her. "Yes, Lieutenant?" That chilly tone again.

"Take us—"

"Past warp 2," he said. "I know."

He worked at his controls. B'Elanna could feel the subtle surge in power as the ship accelerated.

"We're at warp 2.3," Tom reported.

B'Elanna turned to Vorik. "Start emitting the tachyons."

"Energizing the matrix," the Vulcan responded.

"Power is building," Carey announced.

B'Elanna checked her monitor. It didn't seem to her that anything was happening.

"There's no indication of a subspace field," Seven of Nine observed. "I'd recommend switching to a higher energy band."

The lieutenant hated the idea of taking advice from the Borg. Still, Seven of Nine was the expert in this field.

B'Elanna nodded to Vorik. "Do it."

"Yes, Lieutenant."

He switched to the higher band. B'Elanna checked her monitor again. She could see a subspace response.

"That did something," Tom sang out, unable to keep the excitement out of his voice.

"The subspace field is forming," said Seven of Nine.

"Continuing to emit tachyon pulses," B'Elanna noted.

"The field is enlarging," said Seven of Nine.

By then, even the engineer was beginning to enjoy their success. For the moment, all thoughts of the Borg were submerged.

We're going to do it, B'Elanna cheered inwardly. We're going to open that conduit, damn it.

Suddenly, a siren sounded, freezing everyone in engineering. B'Elanna cursed beneath her breath.

"What's that?" asked Seven of Nine.

"An overload alarm," said Vorik.

A moment later, the computer initiated a red alert. The entire section was bathed in a lurid red light.

B'Elanna switched consoles, then keyed the controls. Immediately, she saw what the problem was. She described it for the others.

"There's a power surge in the emitter matrix. Tachyon particles are leaking into the propulsion system."

Tom shouted at Vorik. "Shut down the deflector!"

The Vulcan complied with the order. "Done," he said. His brow creased. "But the leak is continuing unabated."

B'Elanna heard an explosion behind her. Whirling, she saw one of the consoles erupt in a shower of sparks. Her engineers rushed about, attempting to contain the damage.

But it was too late. B'Elanna knew that in a flash, even before *Voyager* began to shudder. This wasn't a broken coolant conduit or something else confined to engineering. This had the makings of a shipwide disaster.

Vorik looked up from his console. "Impulse engines are out."

"Tachyons are flooding the warp core," B'Elanna groaned. "Emissions are increasing exponentially."

Suddenly, Janeway's voice cut through the turmoil. "Bridge to engineering. What's going on down there?"

B'Elanna took a breath. "We've got a power surge in the emitter matrix. Tachyons are flooding the warp core."

"What are the radiometric levels?" asked the captain.

"Fifty rems and climbing," B'Elanna told her.

She imagined Janeway rifling through her options—and rejecting all but one. When the captain spoke, she sounded calm, but there was an undeniable undercurrent of urgency in her voice.

"Listen to me, Lieutenant. If you can't get the core stabilized immediately, evacuate engineering."

B'Elanna didn't like the idea. Unfortunately, she had little choice in the matter. "Aye, Captain. I'll get back to you."

Vorik appeared at her side. "I've cut all power relays, but tachyon levels are still rising."

B'Elanna turned to the other engineers. "Everybody out. Now!"

Her colleagues headed for the door. Vorik went as well. But Tom and Seven of Nine hadn't moved.

"That means you two as well," she told them.

"But I could be of help to you," the Borg noted.

"Get out!" B'Elanna snapped. "That's an order!"

Seven of Nine hesitated a moment, then backed away and left engineering. But Tom stayed where he was, working feverishly at a console.

"You can't order me," he reminded her. "I outrank you, remember?"

B'Elanna didn't argue with him. It wouldn't have gotten her anywhere anyway. "We've got to neutralize the core," she said.

He nodded. "I'll try decoupling the dilithium matrix."

But an ominous whine was beginning to build. Plasma coolant began escaping, just as it had before.

"No effect," B'Elanna growled. "Try it again."

Tom did as she asked. A few seconds later, he shook his head. "It's not working, B'Elanna. The core's going to breach."

She bit her lip. "Let me try one more thing."

Tom grabbed her arm. "B'Elanna, there's no time. We have to get out of here. *Now.*"

The engineer hesitated—but only for a fraction of a second. After all, she knew he was right.

"Computer," she said, "prepare to eject the warp core. Authorization Torres omega-phi-9-3."

The computer responded instantly. "Core-ejection system enabled."

That done, B'Elanna pushed Tom in the direction of the exit and hurried out after him. Once they reached the corridor, she saw the other engineers waiting for them.

First, B'Elanna tapped the control that closed the doors to engineering. Then she steeled herself.

"Computer," she cried out, "eject the warp core."

She couldn't see the core blow out from beneath the ship and tumble away into the void—but, unfortunately, she could imagine it. She couldn't feel *Voyager* listing drunkenly to one side, thanks to the inertial dampers—but she could imagine that, too.

B'Elanna felt as if her own core had been ripped from her. She looked up at the intercom grid.

"Torres to Janeway. We've dumped the core," she reported, feeling a twinge as she said it. After all, it was the last thing a chief engineer wanted to have to say.

"Acknowledged," said Janeway, her voice devoid of emotion. "I'm on my way down, Lieutenant."

B'Elanna looked around at her small, dispirited clutch of engineers. They looked back at her, not knowing what to say.

She saved them the trouble. "Welcome to the worst day of my life."

CHAPTER

15

B'ELANNA STARED AT THE DARK, EMPTY SPACE OCCUPIED by the warp core until just a little while ago. Engineering looked naked to her without the core, like a solar system suddenly deprived of its sun.

Of course, without a sun, the planets in a system would freeze over. Engineering hadn't done that. In fact, the place was busier than ever, with all kinds of personnel assisting in the repair efforts.

Neelix was among them. So was Tom. But not Seven of Nine. B'Elanna had dismissed Tom's new friend. The chief engineer had plenty to worry about without having to keep an eye on a potentially treacherous Borg.

For instance, there was the little matter of getting a propulsion system back on-line. That alone could take hours.

Out of the corner of her eye, B'Elanna saw Captain

Janeway walk into engineering and look around. The lieutenant frowned. Before she got involved in an extended conversation with the captain, she wanted to make sure her key officers had their assignments laid out for them.

"Vorik!" she called. "Carey! Rabinowitz!"

All three of them stopped what they were doing and came over. "How may I be of assistance?" asked the Vulcan.

B'Elanna told him. "We have to get the impulse engines on-line. You and Nicoletti check the driver coils."

Vorik nodded as he retreated. "Yes, Lieutenant."

The chief engineer turned to Rabinowitz, a man with light brown hair and a baby face. "We've got a problem with the microfusion initiators. See if you can trace it to its source."

"Done," the man assured her.

"And while you're at it," B'Elanna told him, "see to the command coordinator. It's a mess."

"On my way," he said.

"And me?" asked Carey.

"Go over the plasma injectors. If they're damaged, they could decide to fire on their own."

"Got it." Carey started to move away.

"When you're done," B'Elanna added, "take a look at the structural integrity field. Blowing out the core could have created some weak spots."

"No problem," Carey assured her, hastening to take care of it—and almost bumping into the captain in the process.

The engineer girded herself. More than anything, she hated the idea of letting Janeway down. After all, the captain had demonstrated faith in B'Elanna from the beginning.

"Report," said Janeway, obviously in no mood for niceties.

"We're stopped cold," B'Elanna told her. "The warp core is millions of kilometers away by now, and the impulse engines are seriously damaged. I can give you a few thrusters . . ."

"But that's it," the captain finished for her.

"That's it," the engineer confirmed.

Janeway frowned. "How long before I can have impulse power?"

B'Elanna shrugged. "I can't give you an estimate. We're still assessing the damage." She sighed. "So much for opening a transwarp conduit. I never thought it was a good idea in the first place."

"No sense in rehashing the past," the captain said pointedly. "What's done is done, Lieutenant."

The engineer nodded. "I sent the Borg back to her alcove. We won't be needing her in here anymore."

Janeway declined to comment on that subject. Instead, she looked around—and stopped when she found what she was looking for.

"Mr. Paris," she called.

Tom raised his head from his console. "Yes, Ma'am?"

"We have to retrieve the warp core," the captain said. "Take a shuttle and find it. See if you can tractor it back to *Voyager.*"

"Yes, Ma'am," said the helmsman. He tapped out a few last commands at his console and started for the door.

"It's going to be damaged," B'Elanna interjected,

getting the captain's attention. "And unstable. It should be repaired before Tom tries to put a tractor beam on it."

Janeway considered the problem for a moment. "All right," she remarked at last. "Then go with him, Lieutenant. Do whatever you have to, just get it back here in one piece."

B'Elanna didn't like the idea of leaving her staff to muddle through without her. But they were capable enough. They would be all right.

"Right away, Captain," she replied.

Then she and Tom headed for the exit.

Lumas stood on his bridge, still dumbfounded by what he had seen. His pilot and his technicians worked all around him, propelling his vessel through space as they took stock of *Voyager*'s largesse.

A Borg, he told himself. A living, breathing Borg, walking the corridors of *Voyager* as if she were just another crew member.

The memory chilled the Caatati to his bones. It left him weak and unnerved. But it also brought with it hot flashes of anger and spite.

If only there were some way to strike at the Borg, Lumas thought. If only he and his ships could seize *Voyager* and remove the devil from their midst. Then she would know what pain was.

And maybe, in the process of exacting his revenge, he would free himself from his *own* pain. Maybe he would achieve some kind of peace by tearing the Borg limb from limb. He tried to picture it . . .

No. He was dreaming if he thought he could capture the Borg. Janeway's vessel was too quick, too well-armed, too powerful for the Caatati. They would gain nothing by converging on *Voyager* except their own annihilation.

"Lumas?" said his second-in-command.

He turned to look at Sedrek. "What is it?"

"We have food for a month, maybe more. And the isotopes they gave us will keep us going even longer than that."

Lumas dismissed the information with a gesture. "They gave us the smallest part of what they had. So what?"

Sedrek shrugged. "I thought you would want to know. You did well."

Lumas glared at him. "If I had done well," he said, "I would have brought you the head of their Borg."

The other man looked at him disbelievingly. "Their Borg? What are you talking about, Lumas?"

"A Borg walked their ship. I swear it. Had I not—"

"Lumas! Come quickly!" called one of his technicians.

Lumas frowned and joined the man at his console. His curiosity aroused, Sedrek came along as well.

"Is something wrong?" Lumas asked. He gazed at the monitor hanging from the bulkhead.

"Not wrong at all," the technician replied. "In fact, it may be something very *right.*" And he pointed to a spot on the monitor.

Lumas took a closer look and saw a red dot tumbling across the screen. "What am I looking at?" he asked.

"I'm not sure," the technician told him. "But it contains some kind of energy—a great *deal* of energy."

Lumas wanted to know more. "Put it on the forward viewscreen."

Then he turned to the hexagonal screen, where the even flow of stars was suddenly displaced by another sight entirely—that of a glowing cylinder plunging end over end through space.

Lumas took a step forward and tilted his head. He had never seen anything like it. "What's its purpose?" he asked.

"It's a power source," the technician responded. "That much is clear. But I can't tell you what it powered."

"*I* can," said another voice.

Lumas glanced over his shoulder at Grommir, another of his technicians. The man was studying the monitor above his console with great intensity.

"It's the energy core from *Voyager*'s main propulsion system," Grommir announced. "Or if it's not, it's an exact duplicate of it."

"How do you know?" asked Lumas.

The technician turned to him. "I scanned *Voyager* and all her systems while the supplies were in transit to us. The signature of this object is a perfect match for *Voyager*'s energy core."

Lumas turned to the viewscreen again. The cylinder was still twirling its way through the void, a treasure beyond description.

"But what is it doing out here?" he wondered.

"That," said Grommir, "I can't tell you."

"Then tell me this," said Lumas, keeping his eyes on the power source. "Can we adapt it to our own needs? Can we make it give us the power we need to survive?"

The technician thought about it. "I suppose so, yes."

Lumas grinned. "Then get a beam on it. I don't care who it belonged to before. It's *ours* now."

Voyager's crew had believed its captain generous, he recalled. It seemed she was more generous than she had intended.

CHAPTER
16

As B'Elanna followed Tom into the shuttlebay, she saw a crew member repairing a burned-out EPS link in one of the bulkheads. Still, the place was a study in decorum compared to engineering.

Tom headed right for the *Cochrane*—his favorite among the ship's several shuttles, though the engineer had forgotten why. He said a few words to Browning, the officer on duty. Then they boarded the craft.

Tom took the controls. After all, he was the hotshot pilot. Besides, B'Elanna was too disgusted with recent events to concentrate.

The bay doors opened and the shuttle slipped easily into space. But she wasn't leaving her troubles behind—far from it.

Crossing her arms over her chest, B'Elanna slouched in her seat. "What else can go wrong today?" she asked out loud.

She hadn't meant to do that. It had just slipped out. Still, it had a positive effect in that it got a smile out of Tom. Not a grin, not a smile that said he enjoyed her company, but a smile nonetheless.

"You know," he said, "you really know how to hurt a guy."

"Yes," B'Elanna answered. "I know." She glanced at him with mock seriousness. "You mean the Klingon in the holodeck, right?"

Her companion glanced back at her, just as mock-serious. "Of course. Who did you think?"

"Just wanted to make sure we understood each other," she told him.

Suddenly, the shuttle vibrated. B'Elanna sat up and looked at her controls. "We're getting close to some random ion turbulence."

Tom nodded. "I'll change course to avoid it."

The crisis past, B'Elanna sank back in her seat. "If we get this core back, I'm going right to bed and sleep straight through until tomorrow. I mean . . ." She heaved a sigh. "I just want to get this day over with."

"Look at it this way," Tom suggested. "How much worse could it get? Having to dump the warp core has to be the low point of *any* day."

She didn't answer—at least, not at first. She just watched the stars fly by at warp 1. At that rate, it would only be a matter of minutes before they found what they were looking for.

"Maybe it's me," B'Elanna speculated. "Maybe I'm asking for all this trouble somehow."

"Or," he said, "maybe it's just a string of bad luck."

She shook her head ruefully. "I never should have

gone through that Day of Honor ceremony. It was ridiculous. No . . . worse than ridiculous."

B'Elanna recalled the sensation of being flat on her back, looking up into the face of her Klingon adversary. She saw his fist, raised and ready to pound her into the cavern floor. I must have been crazy, she thought. Warrior rituals and B'Elanna Torres don't mix.

She attended to some rudimentary tasks on her control console. Still, it didn't take her mind off her misfortunes.

"I shouldn't have gotten *near* anything Klingon," she breathed. "By now, I should know better."

Tom gave her a sidelong glance—but he didn't challenge her, not this time. He looked at his controls instead.

Good, she thought. Because I'm too tired to withstand a challenge. Too tired and too beat up.

Abruptly, Tom's eyes lit up. "Sensors have picked up a polymetallic object. It could be the core."

B'Elanna straightened and worked at her own console. Her findings confirmed her companion's. "That's the warp signature, all right. But there's something else out there. . . ."

"Something else?" he echoed.

She worked at her controls some more. "It's a ship."

It was an ominous thought. Tom looked out the observation port.

"I don't see anything yet," he said.

"We're not in visual range," the engineer advised him. "It'll be a minute or two more."

In the meantime, she did her best to get some information about the ship. She didn't want to confront it without knowing what they were dealing with. But the more data B'Elanna obtained, the less she liked it.

She turned to Tom. "According to our sensors, the ship has the same energy signature as the Caatati."

He met her gaze. "I'm getting a bad feeling about this."

She nodded. "Me, too."

Tom's brow wrinkled. "Maybe they're guarding it for us," he suggested only half-seriously.

B'Elanna frowned at him. "Right. And the Cardassians are really teddy bears in disguise."

A moment later, they came into visual range. "I see it," said Tom.

She followed his gaze, craning her neck to see out the window. "What do they think they're *doing?*" she asked.

There was a narrow shaft of yellow-white energy extending from the Caatati vessel to *Voyager's* warp core. The shaft wasn't holding together well, either—it kept breaking up.

"They're trying to put a tractor beam on it," she snapped. "If they're not careful, they'll rip it apart!"

Tom cursed beneath his breath and opened a communications channel. "This is the shuttle *Cochrane* to the Caatati ship. Please respond."

The Caatati didn't hesitate to respond on audio. "Don't come any closer, *Cochrane*. We're performing a salvage operation."

"What a coincidence," said Tom. "So are we."

"That warp core was ejected from our ship," B'Elanna pointed out. "We've come to retrieve it."

"I'm afraid we got here first," said the Caatati. "Don't interfere with our operation or we'll open fire."

B'Elanna couldn't hold herself back any longer. Arrogance was one thing; stupidity was another.

"Don't you realize that core is highly unstable?" she demanded. "If you try to tractor it like that, you could cause an antimatter explosion."

There was no reply. Tom worked at his console. Then he cursed again, this time more volubly. "They aren't answering."

"Idiots!" B'Elanna snarled.

Tom nodded. "We have to keep them from destroying the core."

B'Elanna thought quickly. Then she got up and went to another control panel at the aft end of the cabin.

"What are you doing?" the helmsman asked.

"I'm going to try to disrupt their tractor beam. Then we can initiate one of our own."

As she manipulated her controls, the shuttle sent out a particle beam. As it met the Caatati beam, the two sizzled and sparked.

Tom checked his sensors. "It's working. Their tractor is breaking down. Pretty soon—"

He was interrupted by a loud thump. Then the shuttle pitched sharply to port and the red-alert lights came on.

B'Elanna felt ice water trickle down her spine. Righting herself in her seat, she checked her monitors again.

"What was that?" Tom asked.

B'Elanna bit back her frustration. "They sent an antimatter pulse back through our particle beam."

"Shut off the beam," he told her.

"It shut *itself* off," she snapped.

The shuttle began shaking. "Warning," said the onboard computer. "The structural integrity field has been compromised."

"Great," said Tom.

"Structural integrity now at fifty-three percent and falling," the computer continued. "Hull breach in one minute, twenty seconds."

B'Elanna worked at her controls. "We've got to reroute power from the propulsion and weapons systems."

"Warning," said the computer. "Hull breach in one minute, ten seconds."

"Do it!" she snapped.

"I'm doing it!" Tom snapped back. "It's having no effect!"

"Warning," the computer declared. "The structural integrity field has collapsed. Hull breach in sixty seconds."

Tom got up and pulled B'Elanna away from her console. "We've got to get out of here!"

She tore away from him. "Where do you suggest we go?"

There was only one place they *could* go, B'Elanna realized. Tom seemed to have come to the same conclusion.

Together, they looked to the rear of the cabin, where the environmental suits were stored. Then they looked at each other again.

"Hull breach in fifty seconds," the computer reminded them.

"Come on," Tom said. "We don't have much time."

Before B'Elanna knew it, he was opening the suit locker and pulling out a suit. Then another. Tom handed her one of them.

The engineer took it with no great enthusiasm. As she began to pull it on over her uniform, she caught a glimpse of her console.

The monitors showed the Caatati ship making off with *Voyager*'s warp core. And there was nothing she or Tom could do to stop it. In fact, they would be lucky to escape with their lives.

"Computer," said Tom, as he pulled on his own suit, "send a distress call to *Voyager*, giving Captain Janeway our coordinates."

Suddenly, a bulkhead panel blew out, releasing a cloud of gas. Then another panel blew, and another. Sparks flew in every direction, blinding B'Elanna with their brilliance.

And the computer wasn't answering Tom's command.

"Computer," he demanded, "respond!"

B'Elanna shook her head as she fastened the last clasp on her suit. "The comm system must be down."

Tom made his way to a console. "Fortunately," he reported, "transporters are still on line."

The shuttle began to shudder, then jerk like a dying beast. The two of them were thrown against a bulkhead.

"Stand by to energize!" Tom yelled over the clamor. Then he reached out and tapped out a command on his control panel.

A moment later, B'Elanna found herself floating in the void of space, her suit protecting her from the harsh realities of the vacuum. She turned and confirmed that Tom was with her.

Then, before she could say or do anything else, a flash of white light caught her eye.

It was the shuttle, she realized. It had been vaporized in the explosion of its destablizing warp core. If she and Tom had waited another second, they would have been vaporized as well.

Of course, their prospects weren't exactly cheery as it was. They were hanging in space, two tiny specks against the infinite—together, of course, but still very much alone.

CHAPTER

17

ONE MOMENT, LUMAS'S VIEWSCREEN SHOWED HIM *VOYAGER's* shuttlecraft amid the customary flickers and lines of static. The next moment, there was a blinding white flash.

Then the screen showed him nothing at all—except stars and static.

He turned to his technicians. "Where did it go?" he demanded. "Where are the people from *Voyager?*"

Grommir was the first to speak. "They're gone."

Lumas stared at him disbelievingly. "Gone?"

"Their ship exploded," the technician explained. "I think it was a result of the antimatter pulse we sent out."

Lumas turned back to the screen. He was so used to aberrations in the thing's performance, he had assumed the shuttle's disappearance was just another technical problem.

But Grommir had indicated otherwise. "Gone," Lumas repeated. He liked the sound of it. He liked it a lot.

That meant the energy core was his—completely and indisputably. If he could beat away one shuttle, he could beat away another one. And without its core, *Voyager* herself didn't scare him much either.

"Wait," said Grommir.

Lumas looked back over his shoulder. "What is it?"

The technician's brow puckered. "For a moment . . ."

"Yes?" Lumas pressed.

Grommir shook his head. "Nothing. I thought something had registered on the sensor grid. It was probably just bits of debris."

Lumas smiled, enjoying his victory. Then he turned to Sedrek. "How is the tractor beam holding up?"

His second-in-command looked up from his console, the glare of his instruments turning his face a lurid red. "It seems to be stable for the moment, Lumas, but we shouldn't use it any longer than we have to. It's a considerable drain on our thorium stores."

His superior made a sound of disgust. "You think too small, Sedrek. With *Voyager*'s energy core in our possession, we'll soon have no need for thorium. We'll have something better."

Then something occurred to him. Maybe Sedrek wasn't the only one guilty of thinking too small. He glanced at Grommir again.

"How long would it take to contact the other Caatati?" he asked.

"Which vessel?" the technician inquired.

Lumas grinned. "All of them."

Grommir looked puzzled. "For what purpose?"

Under normal circumstances, Lumas wouldn't have tendered an explanation. After all, it was *he* who commanded this ship. However, he found himself in an uncommonly generous mood.

"We may have *Voyager*'s core," he pointed out, "but she still has a great many other possessions we could benefit from. Food, for instance. Medical supplies. And other things . . ."

He thought again of the Borg he had seen in *Voyager*'s corridor. He would never forget how she had looked at him. Coldly. Disdainfully.

Entirely without remorse.

"Yes," he said. "A great *many* other things."

B'Elanna stared at the part of space where the shuttle had been. "The captain's going to kill us," she said.

"She's got to find us first," Tom reminded her.

"Which she will, of course. I mean, who *couldn't* find two fully grown people in a place as small as the entire universe?"

Tom quirked a smile. "I'm glad you haven't lost your sparkling sense of humor, Lieutenant."

"No," said B'Elanna, "I guess I haven't. And it's a good thing, because there are few experiences I find more hilarious than watching my warp core ride into the sunset."

He nodded. "Yeah, I kind of enjoyed that myself."

The banter was good, she thought. It helped them

adjust to their circumstances—which were grim at best.

Gazing at Tom through her faceplate, B'Elanna reached out and touched his hand. Looking back at her, he closed his fingers over hers.

It made her feel better. Less isolated, less alone— for all the good it did either one of them.

"As entertaining as this is," Tom said, "it'd be selfish to stay here by ourselves." He pressed a comm pad on his suit. "Paris to *Voyager*. Do you read us? Respond, please. Paris to *Voyager* . . ."

"It's no use," she told him. "The comm system in these suits isn't strong enough to carry that far."

He tried again anyway. "Paris to *Voyager* . . ."

Still nothing.

Tom frowned. "When they get the impulse engines repaired, they'll come looking for us."

"I guess we can't do anything but wait and hope." He managed a smile. "Heard any good jokes?"

She looked at him, wanting very much not to give into pessimism. But despite herself, she sighed.

"What?" he asked.

"You said it couldn't get any worse," B'Elanna reminded him. "You said that dumping the core was about as low as it could go." She looked around them at the vastness of space. "Never figured on this, did you?"

Tom's smile faded. "I will admit that this particular possibility didn't loom large in my mind."

"Still think it couldn't get worse?" she asked him.

"Actually," he said, "the thought that we might run out of oxygen . . . or spring a leak in one of these suits *is* looming large. I guess one of those things would be a little worse."

B'Elanna grunted. "Well, I don't plan on just drifting through space, hoping somebody will come along and rescue us. There must be something we can do to help ourselves."

Tom nodded. "Agreed."

He went silent for a moment. She hoped that meant he was thinking. B'Elanna made an effort to do the same.

"You know," Tom said at last, "if we could interplex the comm systems in both suits, we might be able to create a phased carrier wave. *Voyager* would read the signal and know it's from us."

"Good idea," she told him. In fact, it was a *very* good idea. "Let me access your controls."

He grinned. "I thought you'd never ask."

The two of them pulled closer together until they could grab each other with both hands. Then, in a somewhat more stable position, B'Elanna began fiddling with the controls on Tom's sleeve.

"This would be a lot easier if I had a hyperspanner," she observed.

"It'd be even easier without these gloves," he remarked.

"Hold still . . ."

"I'm trying," he assured her. "Careful we don't lose contact and start drifting apart."

B'Elanna looked at him. Were they still talking about not getting separated in space . . . or something else?

"Right," she replied.

She wrapped one arm around Tom's shoulder to keep him from drifting away as she worked. Then, since that didn't feel secure enough, she hooked her right leg around his left one.

Suddenly, B'Elanna was overwhelmed by the ludicrousness of their situation. Despite the circumstances, she laughed out loud. "I hope no one has us on a viewscreen," she chuckled.

Tom's voice softened. "Tell me, Lieutenant. Why is it we have to get beamed into space, dressed in thick environmental suits . . . before I can initiate first contact procedures?"

The engineer shot him a discouraging look. "Why is it if we're alone for more than thirty seconds, you start thinking about 'contact'?"

He wagged a finger at her. "Not fair, B'Elanna. Not fair at all. The other day in engineering, I must have gone four or five minutes before I started thinking about it."

She scowled at him. Then, with dogged determination, she completed her work. "Okay," she said at last. "I think I've got our comm systems interplexed. I'm going to initiate the carrier wave."

B'Elanna tapped the appropriate controls. Suddenly, there was an earsplitting whine. She could see Tom react in openmouthed shock as the sound filled his helmet.

"Sorry!" she said.

She fiddled with the controls some more. Finally, the whine subsided.

"Better?" she asked.

"Yeah. Was that what your shower sounded like?"

"No," B'Elanna told him. "The shower was worse."

He shook his head. "Let's hope the signal is still that strong by the time it gets to *Voyager.*"

B'Elanna looked around them. "Let's hope," she echoed.

CHAPTER
18

THE CAPTAIN WAS SITTING AT THE DESK IN HER READY
room, reviewing a long list of damage reports. After
all, the ejection of the ship's warp core had had any
number of cascade effects—a disturbing percentage
of them critical to *Voyager*'s operation.

Hearing a chime, Captain Janeway looked up from
her monitor. She had no doubt as to who was on the
other side of the door.

"Come in," she said.

The door slid aside and Seven of Nine walked in.
As before, the Borg didn't say anything. She just stood
there.

The captain got to her feet. "Would you like a cup
of coffee?" she asked. "Perhaps some tea?"

"I have no need to ingest liquids," the Borg informed her. "I still receive energy from the Borg
alcove."

Janeway nodded. Yes, she thought. Of course you do.

"But my understanding is that you're almost ready to begin eating food like everyone else."

Seven of Nine's expression didn't change one iota. Her only response was, "That is what the Doctor says."

"Well, he should know," said Janeway.

Seven of Nine blinked. "Why have you asked me here?"

The captain indicated the informal seating area off to her right, by the observation port. "Please," she said.

The Borg seemed to understand what she meant. As she sat down, Janeway crossed the room and took a seat beside Seven of Nine. Then the captain gathered her thoughts, wanting to be as precise and inoffensive as possible.

"Whenever there's an accident on the ship," she began, "even a minor one, we investigate it. Rather thoroughly, sometimes. That way, we minimize the chances of its happening again."

"A prudent course of action," the Borg remarked.

"I didn't have a chance to talk to Lieutenant Torres before she left the ship," the captain continued. "So I wanted to ask you some questions about what happened in engineering."

Seven of Nine looked unflinchingly at Janeway. "Go right ahead."

The captain didn't hurry. "Sensor logs indicate that tachyons were leaking into the warp core. Do you have any idea how it started?"

"No," said the Borg. "We had reconfigured the deflector shield to emit tachyon bursts, in order to open the transwarp conduits. The procedure must have triggered the leak."

"I see," Janeway said. "And who was controlling the tachyon bursts?"

Seven of Nine didn't hesitate. "Ensign Vorik."

"What were *you* doing?"

"Monitoring the transwarp frequencies."

"And did you at any time access deflector control?"

"No," said the Borg.

"Or maybe disengage the magnetic constrictors?"

Seven of Nine was silent for a moment. "You believe I'm responsible for the accident. That I deliberately sabotaged the ship."

Janeway shook her head. "That isn't what I meant at—"

"But it is," the Borg insisted. "You are like all the others on this ship. You see me as a threat."

The captain's first impulse was to deny the accusation. Then she thought better of it.

"I won't lie to you," she told Seven of Nine. "Part of me is suspicious. We've dealt with tachyon fields before on *Voyager* and never had this problem. And it wasn't so long ago that you made a serious attempt to send a signal to a Borg ship."

"That is true," Seven of Nine conceded.

"But," Janeway went on, "I suspect that if you really wanted to disable this ship, you would have found a much more clever way to do it."

The Borg absorbed the comment. Then she spoke. "Captain, I am unaccustomed to deception. Among the Borg, it was impossible. There were no lies, no secrets in the collective. I do not think that I am capable of fabrication. And I assure you, I had nothing to do with the accident in engineering."

The ball was in Janeway's court. She could slam it back at Seven of Nine or keep the volley going. She chose the latter.

"Thank you," she told the Borg. "I believe you."

Seven of Nine took on a distant look. "I am finding it a difficult challenge to integrate into this group."

The captain nodded. "That's understandable."

"It is full of complex social structures that are unfamiliar to me. Earlier today, I witnessed something called a poker game."

Janeway smiled. "Ah, yes. I'd heard Ensign Kim was trying to start one up. On some ships, it's a tradition."

"A tradition," the Borg echoed.

"Yes. A ritual. Something that gives us comfort over time."

Seven of Nine shook her head. "The Borg have no rituals. No moment is different from any other."

The captain shrugged. "We look at life as more than a series of moments. We try to place them in context, so we can understand them. So we can celebrate them, each in his or her own way."

"That, too, is new to me," said the Borg. "The idea that, in a given situation, in a uniform set of circumstances, each person may act differently."

"It's what makes us individuals," Janeway explained.

The muscles worked in Seven of Nine's jaw. "Compared with the Borg collective, this crew is inefficient and contentious. It lacks discipline and uniformity of purpose."

Janeway sensed that Seven of Nine hadn't completed her thought. "But?" she said softly.

The Borg's brow creased as she considered the matter. "But it is also capable of surprising acts of compassion."

The captain was pleased that Seven of Nine could detect such behavior. "Unexpected acts of kindness are common among our group. That's one of the ways in which we define ourselves."

The Borg seemed to absorb the information. "It is all so different," she breathed. She looked at Janeway. "Is there anything more?"

"There is," the captain told her. "We still have to figure out what caused the tachyon leak." She reached for a padd lying nearby. "Tell me what you remember about the power fluctuations in the propulsion system."

Together, she and the Borg bent to their work.

Paris had forgotten how much he liked floating free in space.

It was invigorating to sit at the conn of a starship and skim through the void, breasting a sea of stars at warp 6. But there was no substitute for swimming that sea on one's own, unfettered and unencumbered, at one with all of creation.

Nor was the universe the immense thing he had once expected it to be. Somehow, when one was drifting through it, one's mind reduced it to a personal space—almost an *intimate* space.

So while someone else might have been frightened by the circumstances in which the flight controller found himself, Paris himself wasn't frightened at all. If he felt anything, it was curiosity.

He turned to B'Elanna, wondering if she felt the same way. Gazing at her faceplate, he could see her eyes darting this way and that, as if she were trying to figure something out.

"How are you doing?" Paris asked.

"This isn't anything like the simulations we had at the academy. I remember them feeling peaceful—"

"Like floating in the womb."

"Yes."

She was getting a queasy look on her face. Clearly, he thought, she wasn't enjoying this as much as he was. He would have to distract her.

"Harry once told me he could remember being in his mother's womb."

No reaction.

"But then," Paris added, "he also told me Susan Nicoletti had a crush on him."

That got B'Elanna's attention. "Why do you say that as though it's ridiculous?"

Paris shrugged. "Well . . . I mean Harry's a great-looking young man and all, or so I've heard . . . but . . ."

"But what?" asked B'Elanna, her nausea apparently forgotten, driven off by indignation. "He's no Tom Paris?"

"It was a long time ago," Paris explained patiently. "But yes, I'd been pursuing Susan rather vigorously, and she wouldn't so much as have a cup of coffee with me."

"And it was *impossible* that she might have taken a liking to Harry instead. Is that what you're saying?"

He frowned. "You're making this sound like something it isn't. I'm not putting Harry down. But at that point, he was naive. Inexperienced. Green, I'd guess you'd say."

"And at that point," B'Elanna noted, "I remember *you*—"

She stopped suddenly. Her queasiness seemed to be coming back.

"I think I'm feeling a little sick to my stomach," she said.

Paris darted to the rescue. "That's because you dropped out of the academy too soon. In the third year there's a six-week program of actual space walks—so you can get used to them."

B'Elanna grunted. "I never would have lasted to the third year. If I hadn't dropped out, they would have asked me to leave."

He chuckled. "I can't believe you were as bad as you say you were."

She scowled. "I was *worse.* Always getting into trouble, arguing . . . fighting. I don't know why they put up with me as long as they did."

"Big, bad B'Elanna. I wish I'd known you then."

She gave him a sidelong glance. "You'd have hated me."

Paris shook his head. "I can't imagine a time when I wouldn't have found you fascinating."

B'Elanna turned to him, not knowing what to say. Obviously, she was unaccustomed to fielding compliments.

Before she could respond, he heard a sound like

comm static. A curtain of light seemed to ripple around them for a moment.

"What the hell was *that?*" Paris wondered.

B'Elanna checked the sensors on her padd. "More ion turbulence," she told him.

Suddenly, he heard something else—a series of shrill alarm beeps. Paris checked his padd and felt a chill climb his spine.

Looking at his companion, he said, "My oxygen supply is leaking."

He'd barely gotten the words out when a computer voice confirmed them. "Warning. Oxygen level at one hundred fourteen millibars and falling."

Paris started pushing controls on his sleeve, but nothing he did seemed to help. "I can't stop it," he groaned.

The computer spoke up again. "Warning. Oxygen level at ninety-three millibars and falling."

B'Elanna looked at him, her face a mirror for his dismay. Then her eyes hardened with resolve. "We'll have to share *my* oxygen."

"Yours?" Paris asked.

"Mine," she confirmed. "It's the only chance you've got."

Before he could protest, B'Elanna pulled him close again. Then she worked at her neck to open a small compartment.

"Warning," the computer voice in the flight controller's suit announced. "Oxygen level at seventy-nine millibars."

Paris could feel his air thinning quickly. He had to draw painfully deep breaths to get what he needed from it.

B'Elanna pulled out an air hose from the vicinity of her neck. Then she attached it to a like compartment in Paris's suit.

"Are you getting air now?" she asked him.

At first, he wasn't. Despite his efforts to remain calm, to breathe evenly, he felt himself gasping, on the edge of panic.

Then, as his lungs filled, he was able to control his breathing better. He was able to relax, at least a little.

"Yeah," Paris rasped. "Much better. Thanks."

"Don't mention it."

B'Elanna turned to the controls on her sleeve—and did a double take. Even through their faceplates, Tom could see the consternation on her face. The *fear*.

"What's wrong?" he asked.

"That turbulence damaged my suit, too," she said. "I should still have at least twenty-four hours' worth of oxygen . . ."

"But?" he prodded.

B'Elanna's face was as devoid of color as he had ever seen it. "But there's only about a half hour left."

Paris cursed beneath his breath. This wasn't good, he thought. This wasn't good at all.

Janeway and Seven of Nine had been at it for over an hour.

They had been sitting side by side in the captain's ready room, making computations on their padds and comparing them, trying to figure out what could have gone wrong with *Voyager*'s attempt to open a transwarp conduit.

To that point, they hadn't found a thing.

Janeway was completing a calculation when Vorik's

voice interrupted her. "Engineering to Captain Janeway."

"Yes, Ensign?" the captain responded.

"I'm pleased to inform you that we are making excellent progress. Impulse power should be restored within the hour."

"Good news," said Janeway. *"Very* good news. Let me know as soon as the engines are on-line again."

"Yes, ma'am."

Just then, Seven of Nine raised her head. "Captain . . ."

Janeway looked into the Borg's eyes and saw a flicker of discovery there. "What is it?" she asked eagerly.

Seven of Nine handed the captain her padd. Janeway took it and studied the figures on it with interest.

"I believe I've found the cause of the accident," said the Borg. "Erratic fluctuations in the ship's warp power output."

"Fluctuations . . ." Janeway muttered.

She saw them now in the midst of all the other information. Unfortunately, they had been within established tolerances, so they hadn't set off an alarm or otherwise called attention to themselves.

"When the tachyon levels rose to a resonant frequency," Seven of Nine explained, "core pressure increased—"

"Exponentially," the captain said. "And the magnetic flow field constricted at the same rate."

The Borg nodded. "Yes."

"Then it *was* an accident," Janeway concluded triumphantly.

She slumped in her seat, relieved. She hadn't

wanted to believe Seven of Nine was responsible for the incident—and now, with the answer in hand, she didn't have to.

Her door chimed, drawing her attention. "Come in," she said.

The door slid aside, revealing Janeway's first officer. He looked worried about something.

"Captain, we just picked up a carrier wave with a Starfleet signature. I'd guess it's Tom and B'Elanna . . . but they're not answering our hails."

Janeway nodded. "They may be in trouble. As soon as we get impulse power back, we'll—"

She never finished her sentence. It was interrupted by Tuvok's intercom voice. "Tuvok to the captain. Can you come to the bridge?"

Janeway exchanged looks with Chakotay, and then with Seven of Nine. "On my way," she replied.

The three of them filed out onto the bridge. Kim, who was manning the ops station, was as serious as Janeway had ever seen him.

Tuvok barked out his report. "We're being approached by an armada of Caatati ships. I count twenty-seven of them."

"They're hailing us," Kim announced.

Janeway turned to the forward viewscreen, wondering what this could be about. "On screen, Mr. Kim."

Abruptly, the Caatati named Lumas appeared on the screen. "Hello, Captain," he said. "We meet again."

"You've brought some friends," she pointed out.

Lumas smiled a hollow smile. "Needy friends, I

fear. We're hoping you will offer us more supplies."

Janeway gathered herself. She could see where this was going. "I made it clear last time that we couldn't possibly provide enough for all your ships. Our resources are limited."

"And I had to accept that, because your ship was more powerful than mine," Lumas told her. "But the situation has changed, hasn't it? You're at a disadvantage now. We have your warp core."

Janeway glanced at Tuvok. He confirmed the boast with a subtle nod. Cursing silently, the captain turned to Lumas again.

"So we both know you can't escape," the Caatati told her. "I'm hoping that will make you . . . shall we say, more generous?"

"I'm afraid you're wrong," the captain told him. "We've given you everything we can spare. Return the core and we'll be on our way."

The Caatati's expression hardened. "We don't really care if you can 'spare' it or not. Prepare to hand over your food, your weapons, and your thorium supply."

"And if we don't?" Janeway asked.

"One of our ships might not seem threatening to you," Lumas noted. "But I assure you, twenty-seven can inflict real damage. And as you've seen, we are desperate. We have very little to lose."

The Caatati let his threat soak in for a moment. The captain didn't take it lightly, either.

"One thing more," he said. "That Borg you're protecting—we want her, too. There are many of us who'd enjoy a chance to repay one of them for what they did to us."

Janeway glanced at Seven of Nine. On the surface, the Borg seemed unmoved. But deep down, where a human still existed in her, she had to be more than a little concerned.

Certainly, the captain was.

CHAPTER
19

B'ELANNA KNEW HOW BAD THE SITUATION WAS. AFTER all, it didn't take an engineer to figure it out.

Half an hour's worth of oxygen had sounded bad. Now she and Tom had even less. Soon, they would have less than that.

Then nothing.

Silence. Fade to black. End of story.

Tom knew what was going on, too. That's why he had been so quiet the last few minutes. Knowing him, he wanted to encourage her, wanted to give her hope—but, obviously, he couldn't find anything to say.

B'Elanna was quiet, too. But then, she had a lot to think about. A lot to deal with. After a while, it seemed like a maze.

Abruptly, Tom pressed the controls on his sleeve.

"I'm cutting the oxygen ratio," he said. "That should give us a few more minutes."

B'Elanna realized she was dozing off. "I'm feeling kind of groggy," she told Tom.

He nodded knowingly. "Oxygen deprivation."

"And you're lowering it?" she asked him.

Tom smiled wanly at her. "Have to try to make it last as long as possible, you know?"

Normally, she would have argued with him. But by then, all the fight had gone out of her.

More silence. They drifted through space, tethered neck-to-neck by B'Elanna's oxygen hose. She ran through the maze some more.

Then something occurred to her, something she felt compelled to share. "It's ironic, isn't it?"

"What is?"

"Today," she said. "The Day of Honor . . . is the day I'm going to die. If only my mother knew."

Tom shook his head emphatically. "We're not going to die, B'Elanna. Stop talking like that."

She grunted. "Just what do you think is going to happen?"

He shrugged. "Anything can happen. Anything at all. And stop arguing—it wastes oxygen."

B'Elanna shot Tom a look, but did as he asked. After all, arguing *would* be a drain on their oxygen supply.

But she couldn't keep silent. Not anymore. "We have to face up to it, Tom. We're going to die."

He frowned. "I don't want to talk about that." Then he glanced in her direction. "There's something I've been wanting to ask you."

"I guess now would be the time."

"When we first met," Tom recalled, "you didn't have a very high opinion of me. Right?"

B'Elanna chuckled. "That's putting it mildly. I thought you were an arrogant, self-absorbed pig."

He smiled. "Flattery won't get you any more oxygen. So . . . now what do you think? Have I changed?"

"A lot," she told him. "Now you're a stubborn, domineering pig."

Tom looked at her, surprised.

"Just kidding," B'Elanna assured him.

Then she realized what she had done. It hit her with the impact of a phaser blast in the stomach.

"There I go again," B'Elanna said, her annoyance evident in her voice. "I'm pushing you away, any way I can. You're right about me, Tom. That's what I do— I push people away."

"Well," he replied, "I'll give you one thing—it's a surefire way of not getting hurt."

She nodded. "You're right." And then, "I'm such a coward."

"No, you're not."

"I am," she insisted.

Tom wrapped his arm around her. "Shhh. Save your air."

But she couldn't stop talking, couldn't stop facing things she hadn't wanted to face before. "Funny. Now I wish I'd finished the Day of Honor ritual, even though I wasn't faring too well. At least if I'd seen it through, maybe I'd feel . . . I don't know. Complete."

"Complete?" he echoed.

She was having trouble putting the right words

together. It was the lack of oxygen—she knew that. Still, it was frustrating.

"I don't know what I'm trying to say," she told Tom. "All my life, this has all been so confusing—this Klingon business. My mother, my father. It's always been easier just to ignore it."

"Until I dredged it up," he interjected.

B'Elanna nodded. "Until you dredged it up." She looked at Tom. "No, that's not fair. Not fair at all. I've spent my life running from who I am. All you've done is help me stop and turn around. And now that I have . . ."

Suddenly, she was overcome with emotion.

"And now that you have?" he prodded.

B'Elanna heaved a sigh. "It's too late."

Anger flared in Tom's eyes. "Stop that."

She shook her head. "We have to look at it, Tom. We have to stop kidding ourselves. If I'm going to die, I want to acknowledge it. Maybe there are things that . . . that should be said."

He gave her a long, searching look. "Maybe so," he agreed.

"Don't you have any regrets?" B'Elanna asked. "Things you'd like to get off your chest?"

Tom laughed softly. "Too many to list."

She held his gaze with her own. "Why not start?"

The flight controller hesitated. The conversation had unexpectedly turned back on him, and he was clearly no more comfortable talking about himself than B'Elanna was.

"I wish my parents could know me now," he said. "My father especially. I wish he could see me wearing a Starfleet uniform again. I guess that's my main regret." He looked at her. "How about you?"

B'Elanna pondered the question. "I wish . . . I wish I knew my father better. I was only five when he left us. One day I came home and he was making arrangements to ship out—just like that."

Tom looked sympathetic. "Sometimes those things just happen."

Silence again. All B'Elanna could hear was the sound of her breathing, harsh and labored.

"Feel better?" asked Tom.

"You?" she countered.

He thought for a moment. "I guess so."

B'Elanna nodded. "Me, too."

Janeway glared at the viewscreen. Lumas's image had disappeared, leaving her and her officers with a view of the nearly thirty Caatati vessels amassed against them.

She wondered if Rahmin's ship was among them. She wanted to think that it wasn't, but she couldn't know for certain.

"Our weapons are a lot more powerful than theirs," Chakotay pointed out. "I say we put up a fight."

Tuvok frowned. "Perhaps they will settle for less than they demanded. It is a common bargaining strategy."

Kim agreed. "Maybe if we give them *something*, it'll appease them."

Janeway shook her head. "Given the mood the Caatati are in now, I can't imagine what would satisfy them—short of all we have."

"I will go," said the Borg, who had been silent to that point.

All heads turned. Seven of Nine met their gazes evenly.

"They asked for me," she pointed out. "If I surrender myself, perhaps they will let you leave."

Janeway stared at her. It was the first altruistic gesture she had ever heard from a Borg. In that sense, it was as remarkable as any cosmic phenomenon she had ever been fortunate enough to witness.

"Seven," the captain said, "that's very generous of you. And very courageous. But I will *not* turn you over to them."

The Borg tried to absorb Janeway's remark. "I was only offering to do what would be best for this group," she explained.

The captain smiled. "You're *part* of this group now. And we're going to protect you, one way or the other."

Seven of Nine's brow puckered. Clearly, she was struggling to understand this ethic.

"You . . . want to protect me?"

Janeway nodded. Then she turned to the others.

"It's time to stop talking about this," she said. "Tom and B'Elanna are in trouble and we have to find them. Tuvok?"

"Yes, Captain."

"What's the status of our weapons array?"

The Vulcan's answer was quick and to the point. "Weapons are at the ready. However, our shield strength is extremely low."

Janeway considered that. "We can shut down non-essential systems. Reroute power to the shields." She looked around the bridge at her officers. "We're going to fight."

"That might not be necessary," declared Seven of Nine.

She seemed excited—or perhaps agitated. It was difficult for the captain to tell which.

In any case, Janeway dismissed the suggestion. "I've already said that giving you up is not an option."

"I am referring to another strategy," the Borg told her.

"In that case," said Janeway, "let's hear it."

"Caatati technology," said Seven of Nine, "depends on thorium isotopes. That is what drives their ships. It is what powers their systems. If they had enough thorium, they could become self-sustaining."

"But we don't have that much thorium to give them," Kim reminded her. "In fact, we have very little."

Seven of Nine had an answer for him. "When we assimilated the Caatati, the survivors lost their ability to replicate the isotopes. But I have retained that knowledge. I could design an energy matrix which would produce thorium in large quantities."

Janeway realized her mouth was open. She closed it.

"Seven," Chakotay asked, "if you had this knowledge all along, why didn't you say something?"

The Borg hesitated. She seemed almost annoyed. "I am not accustomed to thinking that way. Borg do not consider giving technology away. They only think of assimilating it."

When the captain spoke, it was in her gentlest tone. "And what do you suppose made you consider it now?"

Seven of Nine turned to her, clearly at a loss. "I am not certain."

"Maybe," the captain suggested with a certain satisfaction, "it was just an unexpected act of kindness."

The Borg pondered that possibility. "Maybe," she allowed at last.

Clearly, Seven of Nine had a long road to travel before she could call herself human again. However, in Janeway's eyes, she had taken a big step along that road.

Progress, the captain thought. It was nice to see.

"Let's go," she said to all and sundry. "Seven, you work with Vorik to build the energy matrix, while I convince the Caatati there's a better way out of this than bloodshed."

As Janeway watched the Borg head for the turbolift, she was already choosing the words she would use to pitch the deal to Lumas.

CHAPTER
20

JANEWAY WATCHED LUMAS'S REACTION ON THE VIEW-screen. Obviously, he hadn't expected a counteroffer.

"A limitless supply of thorium isotopes?"

"That's what I said," the captain told him. "Imagine, never having to beg for them again. Imagine never having to beg for *anything*."

The Caatati made a derisive sound. "It's impossible."

"What if it's not?" she rejoined.

Lumas's eyes narrowed. "You're trying to deceive me."

"If that were the case," Janeway declared, "would I have picked such an outlandish premise?"

Actually, she thought, I might have. But he doesn't know me well enough to realize that.

The Caatati still wasn't buying it. "How is it you never mentioned an energy matrix before?"

"I didn't know there was such a thing," the captain replied honestly. "It was suggested to me only a few minutes ago."

Lumas looked at her askance. "Then how do you know it will work?"

"Actually," said Janeway, "I don't. But if I were you, I'd be willing to exercise a little patience to find out. Then, if it turns out we can't come up with the matrix after all, you haven't lost a thing. You can still use your greater numbers to try to pound us into submission."

Though I'd still put my credits on *Voyager,* the captain mused. But she kept her sentiment to herself.

The Caatati considered her proposition. "How long do you need to create the matrix?" he asked at last.

"An hour," she told him.

He chuckled dryly, thinking Janeway was joking. "That's all?"

The captain smiled. "That's what *I* said."

Lumas watched Janeway's image vanish from his viewscreen. Once again, he found himself looking at *Voyager*'s predicament—that of a single starship surrounded by a swarm of Caatati vessels.

Sedrek approached him. "Captain Janeway says she can give us all the thorium we need."

"That's what she says," Lumas agreed.

"Can we believe her?" Sedrek asked.

Clearly, he hoped that they could. It showed in his eyes and in the way the muscles rippled in his temples.

Lumas shrugged. "Perhaps. But even then . . ."

His second-in-command looked at him. "Yes?"

"I need some time alone in my quarters," said Lumas. "I have a great deal to think about."

Sedrek seemed to understand. "And in the meantime?"

"If *Voyager* makes a move," Lumas told him, "let me know. Otherwise, simply maintain our position."

The other man nodded. "Understood."

Lumas clapped him on the shoulder. Then he left the bridge and retired to his cabin. After all, he *did* have a great deal to think about.

As the door to his cabin irised open and Lumas looked inside, he was struck by how small his quarters looked. How cramped and confined.

But then, his perspective had changed. Lumas was seeing the place with eyes that Janeway had opened to new vistas—new possibilities. And not just for him, but for his long-suffering people.

Certainly, the prospect of being able to generate thorium isotopes whenever necessary was an attractive one. It would mean an end to poverty, an end to sickness and hunger. It would mean the Caatati could again devote their lives to something besides survival.

But Lumas had yet to see proof of Janeway's claims. He had yet to see her miracle machine with his own eyes.

And if she showed it to him? he asked himself. If she demonstrated it could do everything she had said it could?

Then what?

Was he to embrace it without reservation—and in doing so, embrace the insidious deal the human had set before him? Was he to forget all the misery and devastation his people had endured and let the Borg witch go free?

Lumas shook his head. He couldn't do it. He couldn't forget what the Borg had done to him. Even if it meant the death of his people, even if it meant the extinction of the entire Caatati race, he couldn't let a chance for revenge slip through his fingers.

He would tell Janeway that he rejected her proposition. And if she remained steadfast in her refusal to turn over the Borg, he would carry out his threat. He would set his ships on her like a pack of sharp-toothed *g'daggen* on a fat-laden *quarril*.

Either way, the Borg would have occasion to regret what her race had done. Either way, she would—

"Father?" came a voice.

Astounded, Lumas turned to look back over his shoulder. He saw his daughter Finaea standing there. She looked concerned.

"You're unhappy, father. Do you want to talk about it?"

For a moment or two, he didn't understand. Then his fingers climbed to the crown of his head and felt the cool, slender form of the realizor there.

"I don't remember—"

"Remember what?" asked Finaea, smiling gently at her father's confusion.

I don't remember putting on the realizor, he mused, finishing the thought. But he didn't tell his daughter that, because it would also have meant telling her she wasn't real—and she had endured enough pain.

Lumas smiled back at her. "I didn't remember seeing you come in. That's all." He reached for her hand and held it. "Where are your mother and your sister? At the marketplace?"

Finaea seemed to look more deeply into his eyes than ever before. "They didn't come because . . . because they couldn't," she explained.

"Couldn't?" he echoed.

Lumas didn't understand. After all, his wife and daughters *always* came together, except on those rare occasions when he preferred the company of only one or two of them.

Finaea paused, as if searching for words. "You needed to talk," she said finally. "With me. *Just* with me."

He felt a chill climb the rungs of his spine. "How would you know that?" he asked softly.

She shrugged. "I'm part of you, Father. I always have been. And right now, I'm the part you need the most."

Lumas looked at her with dread in his heart. The way Finaea was speaking to him, it was almost as if she knew . . .

No, he insisted. That was impossible. She wasn't real. She had no awareness except for his awareness, no reality except that which—

—that which he *gave* her.

Suddenly, Lumas figured out what must have happened. As he sat there pondering Janeway's offer, he had unknowingly taken hold of the realizor and placed it on his head—and entirely without meaning to, he had conjured up the image of his daughter Finaea.

Yes, he thought. That was it.

And because she had come from his subconscious

mind, she wasn't the Finaea that he knew and loved. Or rather, not *just* that Finaea. This one was aware of herself as a construct. She knew that she was there for a reason.

And that reason was . . . to assure him he had made the right decision? Or to argue against it? There was only one way to find out, he supposed.

"You know of the human captain's proposal," Lumas said.

It felt strange speaking to his daughter of such things—so strange, in fact, he thought about replacing her with the Finaea he remembered. But in the end, he didn't.

"I know of it," she confirmed.

"Then you also know I've decided to reject it."

Finaea regarded him. "You'll destroy *Voyager?*"

"Only if necessary," he told her. "More than likely, Janeway will give up the Borg first. And even if she doesn't, there's no reason to annihilate the ship—not when we can strip it for its resources."

"I see," said his daughter. "And this is just. After all, the Borg destroyed our homeworld, through no fault of our own."

"Exactly," Lumas replied.

"And you'll take no joy in battering and stripping *Voyager,*" Finaea went on. "It's not as if you mean the captain and her crew any harm. You're just doing what you have to in order to survive."

"That's right," he responded, relieved that Finaea had the sense to see things his way.

She nodded. "Just like the Borg."

Lumas felt as if he had been dealt a physical blow. He shook his head from side to side. "No," he said.

"Not at all like the Borg. I'm not a coldhearted murderer, Finaea. You know me better than that."

"But you would sooner kill innocent people than let a Borg go free."

"I'm doing it for you!" he told her. "For you! The Borg took my family away and made monsters out of them! If I have a chance to strike back at them, how can I ignore it?"

His daughter looked at him as lovingly as she had ever looked at him in life. "You can ignore it," she said, "because you're *not* like them. When the Borg took me and mother and Anyelot, they turned us each into one of them. But it'll be a greater tragedy if they turned *you* into one of them, too."

Lumas's throat hurt. He swallowed hard and fell to his knees at Finaea's feet. Tears streamed down his cheeks—just as they had his last day on the Caatati homeworld.

"They took you away from me," he moaned. "They took you all. And there was nothing I could do about it."

Lumas felt a hand on his shoulder. Looking up, he saw that his daughter was smiling down at him. "It's all right," she said. "I forgive you, Father." And then again: "I forgive you."

They embraced. And they stayed that way for a long, long time.

CHAPTER
21

As Lumas took his place on the bridge of his ship, every technician there turned to look at him. Sedrek was no exception.

After all, they knew what kind of decision he had to make. What's more, they knew how important it could be to them—and to all Caatati.

On the viewscreen, nothing had changed. *Voyager* was still surrounded by the force Lumas had assembled.

"Contact Janeway," he said.

One of his technicians worked at his controls for a moment. "I've established a communications link," the man reported.

Lumas nodded. "On screen."

A moment later, Janeway's face appeared. "Hello again. I take it you've had enough time to consider our offer?"

"I have," he confirmed.

The human regarded him. "And?"

"I want to see this matrix of yours. Is it ready?"

"It is," Janeway told him. "And I'll be glad to show it to you." She gave an order to someone offscreen, then looked to the Caatati again. "If you lower your shields, we'll beam you over."

Then her image vanished and was replaced by that of her vessel. Sedrek came to stand by Lumas.

"Are you sure about this?" he asked. "What if they open fire once our shields are down? Or try to make a hostage out of you?"

Lumas shook his head. "They won't try either— not with so many Caatati ships surrounding them."

"All the more reason to destroy us—or take you hostage," his second-in-command argued. "They know you're the one who brought the Caatati together. With you out of the way . . ."

Lumas dismissed the idea with a gesture. "You flatter me," he said. "I am no more important than anyone else, Sedrek. There are any number of commanders here who can lead an assault as well as I can."

The Caatati didn't believe that, of course. It just seemed like the right thing to say.

He turned to Grommir. "Lower shields."

Reluctantly, the technician did as he was told.

Lumas took a breath, then let it out. Before he had finished exhaling, his surroundings had changed. He found himself standing in a large room full of complex equipment.

He wasn't alone, either. Janeway was there.

And so was the Borg.

Janeway watched Lumas's face as he materialized in engineering.

The Caatati noticed her first. Then he turned and saw that Seven of Nine was present as well, and his eyes widened.

"The Borg . . ." he said.

"Her name is Seven of Nine," the captain told him. "And she's the one who designed the energy matrix for you."

She indicated the device, a globe with a flat surface at each of its poles. It was rather small, considering the magnitude of its importance to the Caatati. Lumas tore his eyes away from the Borg and studied it.

But he was still thinking about Seven of Nine. Janeway could see it in his expression, in the way the muscles in his temples fluttered. He was thinking about what the Borg had done to his people.

Allowing Seven of Nine to present the matrix was a calculated risk. The captain had known that at the outset. However, she wanted Lumas to see that the Borg wasn't the monster he imagined her to be.

Not anymore. Now she was simply another member of *Voyager's* crew. And without Seven of Nine— without her knowledge and experience—Janeway could never have offered the Caatati the hope of prosperity.

"This matrix," said the Borg, "will produce nine hundred and forty-four grams of thorium per day."

Lumas took a closer look at the energy device. He gave the impression that he was qualified to understand its workings, though Janeway wasn't at all sure that was the case.

"Now you can power all your systems," the captain told him, "and begin to rebuild your replication technology. You can feed all those children you spoke of." She let that tantalizing prospect hang in the air for a moment.

The Caatati looked up—not at Janeway, but at Seven of Nine. "You think this makes up for what you've done?"

"It can't," said the captain. "Nothing can. But as you can see, this woman is no longer part of the Borg collective. She has changed. And if she can do it, perhaps you can, too."

Lumas eyed her. "It's easy for you to say that. It wasn't your family her people killed."

Janeway sighed. "I haven't lost family to the Borg—but I've lost friends and colleagues. My people have experienced their share of misery at the hands of the collective."

The Caatati seemed surprised by that. "And you don't hate them?" He glanced at Seven of Nine. "You don't hate *her?*"

"I hate what they've *done,*" said the captain. "But I can't hate *them* any more than I can hate a planet for orbiting its sun. Remember—every Borg was a victim before he became an aggressor. Every one of them was plucked from the heart of a civilization he loved. And in that regard, Seven of Nine is no exception."

And neither, Janeway thought, was any loved one Lumas had lost to the Borg invasion. She hadn't come out and said that, hoping the Caatati could make that leap of logic for himself.

"Will you call off your armada and allow us to leave?" she asked.

Lumas frowned. "One device isn't enough for all our ships."

"True," said Seven of Nine. "But using this matrix as a template, you can construct as many matrices as you like. We can provide you with all the necessary components and specifications."

Lumas stared at her. Somewhere inside him, a struggle was taking place. The captain imagined she understood part of that struggle, but not all of it.

After all, she knew so little about the Caatati, and even less about Lumas himself. She could only hope her words had made some sense to him.

Because if they hadn't, the future looked bleak indeed. But not for the Caatati—for Janeway and her crew.

Lumas picked up the matrix and hefted it in his hands. Then he turned to the captain, his expression a difficult one to read.

"You're free to go," he told her. "And . . . thank you."

The captain smiled. She was about to respond to Lumas's expression of gratitude when the Borg did it for her.

"You're . . . welcome," said Seven of Nine.

The Caatati looked at her. Obviously, he hadn't expected that.

Neither had Janeway. She regarded the Borg in a new and more hopeful light. Progress, she thought. And just in the nick of time.

* * *

B'Elanna sighed in the confines of her mask.

She wanted to see her father one last time. She wanted to ask him what he had been doing with his life the last twenty years or so.

She wondered if he was happy—if he was glad that he had gone his own way. If he ever missed his Little Bee.

After all, she hadn't heard from him since that day he left the colony. Not even once. He had promised her he would visit all the time, and keep in touch via subspace packet. But he hadn't.

And when B'Elanna pleaded with her mother for an explanation, her mother told her that was how humans were. *Some* humans, anyway.

Her father was alive and well, her mother said—she knew that for a fact. But if he didn't care enough about his daughter to stay in touch, he was to be forgotten—treated as if he were dead.

Of course, her mother was a Klingon, the offspring of a prominent house. To such a woman, pride was everything. Pride and that stiff-necked sense of honor she was famous for.

As a child, B'Elanna had always hated those qualities in her mother. She had always blamed them for driving her father away.

And maybe they had.

But looking back now, she saw that they were part of her mother—part of what made her what she was. And part of her mother's half-Klingon daughter, too, no matter how hard she tried to deny it.

What a mess I am, B'Elanna thought. On one hand, looking for love—and on the other, pushing it away as hard as I can. On one hand, seeking approval—and on the other, resisting it.

Maybe her mother had had the right idea. Maybe she had been more courageous than . . . courageous than . . .

"Warning," said a voice.

B'Elanna started at the sound. It was only then that she realized she had begun to doze off.

"Oxygen level at one hundred four millibars and falling," said the computer in Tom's suit.

B'Elanna shook him. Tom's eyelids fluttered, but didn't open. Apparently, his slumber had been deeper than hers.

"Tom," she said, her voice thick and a little slurred. It was getting harder and harder to speak, much less make herself understood.

"Mmmm," was his only response.

"Tom," she said again, this time with more urgency.

"Leave me alone," he replied, like a child telling his mother he was too tired to go to school that morning.

"Come on," she insisted. "Open your eyes."

He squinted at her. "I was having a dream. A really nice dream. We were home. There were lots of people cheering and pinning medals on us." He smiled happily. "Don't be afraid, B'Elanna. It's not going to be hard. It's going to be really . . . peaceful."

"Warning," said the computer in Tom's suit. "Oxygen level at eighty-seven millibars and falling."

B'Elanna believed what Tom had told her. In the end, it would be peaceful. But she couldn't face the end. Not just yet.

"Tom, there's something I have to say . . ."

"Me, too," he said. "I'm glad the last thing I'll see . . . is you. . . ."

B'Elanna found herself pulling Tom closer, environmental suit and all. He was pulling her closer as well. And it wasn't just the fact that neither of them wanted to die alone.

"No," she told him. "Something else . . ."

"What?" Tom asked softly.

It was hard for B'Elanna to remain focused. She was so light-headed, the words seemed to dissipate and drift off into oblivion. But her determination won out.

"I've been a coward," she confessed. "About everything. Everything that really matters."

"You're being a little hard on yourself," he said dreamily.

"No," B'Elanna declared. "I'm going to die— without a shred of honor. And for the first time in my life, that bothers me. So I have to tell you something. I have to—"

"Warning," Tom's computer interrupted. "Oxygen level at seventy-one millibars and falling."

Tom's eyes were closing.

"Tom," B'Elanna said.

He came awake with a start. "I'm here," he told her. "It's okay. It won't be long now."

"I have to tell you the truth," B'Elanna said. "Maybe then I can die with a little honor after all."

"Truth about . . . about what?" he asked.

"Something I haven't said before," she sighed. "So at least, I won't pile up any more regrets."

B'Elanna swallowed. It was harder than she'd thought it would be.

"If I . . . if I didn't know we were dying . . . I could never say this." She smiled. "Silly, isn't it?"

"Warning," said Tom's suit computer—like the knell of doom. "Oxygen level at six-two millibars and falling."

"Better say it now," Tom told her. "We don't have much longer . . ."

"Okay," B'Elanna said. "Okay." She looked into his heavy-lidded eyes. "It was all for you, Tom."

He seemed puzzled. "For me?"

"All for you," she repeated. "The Klingon rituals, the Day of Honor. I just wanted you to be proud of me."

Tom shook his head. "You didn't have to . . . to do anything to make me proud, B'Elanna. I was proud . . . of you already. . . ."

It was so *frustrating*. Why couldn't she just come out and say it? "No, you don't understand . . . what I'm trying to say . . ." She took a deep, ragged breath and got it out.

Finally.

"I love you, Tom."

He didn't answer. He just looked at her, stunned by her admission and losing consciousness from lack of oxygen.

"Well," B'Elanna said at last, "say something."

Tom gave her a weak smile. "You picked a great time to tell me . . ." Then his eyelids began to flutter dangerously. "To tell me . . ."

As his eyes closed, a peaceful look came over him. B'Elanna's secret revealed, she felt a great burden fall away from her. Maybe it was time to let her eyes close as well, she thought.

And they did.

But not before she hugged Tom as hard as she could. And somehow, even though he was all but unconscious, he hugged her back.

B'Elanna's last thought was that Tom was right. It *was* peaceful dying this way. And their being together made it even more so.

But something wouldn't let her go. At first, she didn't know what it was, but it kept tugging at her, insisting that she pay heed to it.

She opened her eyes.

"My god," B'Elanna whispered.

There was something in the distance. Something bright and shiny. It was too far away for her to make out its shape, but it hadn't been there before. And unless she was completely crazy, it was getting larger.

Suddenly, another voice came to her. Not the computer voice they'd been listening to, measuring the time left to them. No, this was a different voice. A more welcome voice.

"Voyager to Tom Paris. This is the captain, Tom . . . do you read me? Respond. *Voyager* to B'Elanna Torres. This is the captain . . ."

Tom's eyes came open again. He looked around, dazed. Then he licked his lips and spoke in a voice so low, B'Elanna could barely hear it. "We're here . . . Captain . . . we're here . . ."

Janeway's voice soared with joy. "We were beginning to get worried about you. Prepare to beam aboard."

B'Elanna smiled. Then she turned to Tom. She looked at him, searching his face for whatever emotion she might find there.

Tom looked back at her, doing the same thing. But even she didn't know what he saw.

B'Elanna knew only one thing for certain—nothing would ever again be the same between them. She was still holding on to that thought as the familiar confines of the transporter room appeared around them . . .

Nothing would ever again be the same.

EPILOGUE

THE DOCTOR WAS IN HIS OFFICE, THINKING ABOUT ALL that had happened to him in the last several hours, when he received a communication over the ship's intercom system.

"Doctor, this is Commander Chakotay. I have a couple of patients for you."

"I see," said the Doctor. "And who might these patients be?"

"Lieutenants Paris and Torres. We've just recovered them. Seems they were a bit low on oxygen."

"Bring them in," the Doctor advised him. "At the very least, someone should take a look at them."

"They're on their way," said Chakotay.

The Doctor approached the nearest biobed and waited patiently for Torres and Paris to arrive. Another day, he thought, another holiday.

He couldn't wait to celebrate.